FRANKIE!

ALSO BY WILANNE SCHNEIDER BELDEN

Mind-Call

Mind-Hold

The Rescue of Ranor

FRANKIE!

Wilanne Schneider Belden

Illustrated by Stewart Daniels

HARCOURT BRACE JOVANOVICH, PUBLISHERS
San Diego   New York   London

HBJ

Text copyright © 1987 by Wilanne Schneider Belden
Illustrations copyright © 1987 by Stewart Daniels

Requests for permission to make copies of any part of the work
should be mailed to:
Permissions, Harcourt Brace Jovanovich, Publishers,
Orlando, Florida 32887.

Library of Congress Cataloging-in-Publication Data
Belden, Wilanne Schneider.
Frankie!
Summary: The O'Riley family is far from normal,
since it includes a wizard, a magician, and an
apprentice witch, and they are delighted when
Mother's next baby turns out to be a griffin.
[1. Griffins—Fiction.   2. Magic—Fiction.
3. Fantasy]   I. Title.
PZ7.B38882Fr 1987   [Fic]   86-33507
ISBN 0-15-229380-9

Designed by Frankie M. Smith

Printed in the United States of America

First edition

A B C D E

To the memory of my father, Bill Schneider, who told me stories of Teeny and Weeny, the two little chipmunks, when I was so young I thought they were true

Contents

FRANKIE!

Griffins
in the Family?

A STORY BY BRIDGIT O'RILEY

I was almost eight years old before I found out that we have griffins in our family. One morning at breakfast, Mother told Mike, Pat, and me that she was going to have a baby.

"Please have a girl, Mother," I pleaded. "I really need a sister." It was hard enough having three younger brothers. Four would be impossible!

"Suppose it'll be a griffin this time, Kathie?" Daddy wondered.

"A what?" the boys asked.

"A griffin," Mother repeated. "It could be."

"What's a griffin?" Mike asked.

I was glad he asked. I had an idea, but it was so silly that it couldn't be right.

"Griffins are Magical creatures," Daddy explained. "Most of them are in Magic." He meant the place. "There aren't but one or two in the Real World at any one time. All those born into Real belong to your mother's family—yours, too. Did you know you belong to the last truly Magical family in the Real World?"

"*Mother* isn't magical," Pat protested.

"Not herself. But she has the genes. Any of her children can be. What about you, old wizard-to-be?"

That quieted Pat for a minute. At least he had to think about it.

"*What is a griffin?*" Mike almost shouted.

Nobody paid any attention to him.

"But if there are *any* griffins in Real, why don't we see them or hear about them or something?" I wanted to know.

"There used to be many of them, thousands of years ago when everyone believed in Magic," Daddy answered. "They disappeared when people stopped believing—or began believing all Magic was evil."

"When was the last one in Real?" Pat asked.

"When I was a little girl," Mother answered, "and, occasionally, since. I have a griffin-brother—Francis. He's the Uncle Fran we talk about—the one you've never met."

"He's a griffin?" I couldn't believe it.

Daddy nodded. "He is, indeed. The last time he was in Real was when your mother and I were married."

"But . . ." I began.

"A great honor," Daddy went on. "He didn't come to any of your aunts' or uncles' weddings."

"He told me it was because Daddy's a real Magician," Mother put in. "He felt comfortable."

"Which was more than anybody else did!" Daddy shook his head and began to laugh.

Mike tried again. Shouting hadn't worked, so he asked very quietly, "But Daddy, what *is* a griffin?"

"Shall we take pity on him?" Daddy asked Mother.

She grinned and nodded.

He got up. "I've some pictures of Fran that were taken at the wedding. Where's the wedding album, Kathie?"

"Bottom drawer of my desk, I think," she said.

"I'll get it."

While he was gone we finished breakfast and cleared up. Mother wiped off our littlest brother, Dennis, and put him down in his play-pen. Daddy seemed to take at least a week.

"Ah-ha!" he said, looking into the album as he came back into the dining room. "Here they are." He put the open album on the table, and we all crowded around.

In all the pictures on that page was a huge beast. It had the head, wings, and forelegs of an eagle, the body and back legs of a lion, and the tail of a snake.

"But that's not a person," Mike yelped. "How could we have one of those things in the family?"

"I don't understand, either," I said. "Mother, how could you have a griffin? Birds hatch baby birds, dogs have puppies, and people have baby people."

"Correct, Bridgit!" Daddy acted as if I'd just stated Rule One of the Laws of the Universe.

Now I knew he'd been kidding all along.

"Oh, Daddy!" I was pretty disappointed. I didn't know how he'd managed the pictures, but he is a Magician, so it shouldn't have been very hard.

Pat and Mike and I all looked at each other. Pat and I were thinking the same thing, and I knew Mike must have been, even if he can't mind-talk. We started out of the room together.

Daddy is the Magician in our family. I'm learning to be a Witch. Pat was born with something so special we're a little scared of it. He'll be a Wizard when he grows up. Denny's too little to know about yet. But Mother? Mother can't even mind-talk. If being Magical was what it took, Mother could never have a griffin.

"Children," Mother said in her tone of voice that means "I'm sorry, come here and let me explain." We looked at each other again, then turned and went back.

"I may not be personally Magical, any more than Mike is—which is reasonable, as he's like me. But my ancestors and several of my family are Magical. It's heredity, children," Mother said. "You'll learn more about it in school. It means that even though I'm not Magical myself, my children can be. And are. Bridgit and Pat."

"It's not because Daddy's a Magician?" I asked. "I always thought it was."

"I'm sure that helps," Mother said. "But it's not necessary."

"Mother," Mike put in, "if Pat and Bridgie are, why am I not?"

"Heredity, again. And pretty complicated. But most of your cousins aren't, either. Much of the Magic in your generation is right here in this room."

"There are more of us than there are of them?" Mike asked.

"Um-hm."

"It's not fair."

"I know, Michael. I didn't think it was either, when I was growing up. But we're necessary. You'll find out one day that you don't mind. I don't. Being us is just as good." She reached out and hugged him. I don't think he agreed, but he didn't pull away.

"So you could have a griffin?" Pat asked, getting back to the subject.

"Yes."

"How?" I was very confused.

"It wouldn't start out as a griffin, Bridgit. In Real, griffins are born as perfectly normal babies. But they soon begin to change. By the time they're seven hours old, they've turned into horrible monsters."

"Horrible monsters?"

"Well, that's what they'd look like to most people."

"Oh."

None of us said anything for a while. Then Mike ventured, "What's it like having a griffin for a brother?"

"Marvelous! He flies, of course, and breathes fire like a dragon. He knows where to find lost things, where people are, who's doing what—

all sorts of useful things. Griffins grow up in those seven hours until they're like seven-year-old children. They learn to talk even faster than speedy old Pat."

My second brother learned to talk as well as a five-year-old by the time he was two. It really upset people.

"Their rate of growth and development slows down a bit for four or five years. But they also become Magicians and can do all sorts of Magical things."

"How big do they get?"

Mike didn't have to be a telepath to tell me what he really meant. He's the adventurous athlete in the family. Just the word *flies* would be enough for him.

"Oh, as large as they want to be," Daddy said.

All three of us looked at him.

"When he gets big, can you ride on him?"

I don't suppose I was the only one who noticed that "griffins" in general had become "he."

Mother chuckled. "You certainly can."

Mike pulled away from Mother's arm. We three all looked at the pictures in the album again. This time I noticed that the eight-foot-tall griffin was wearing a top hat, bow tie, and spats, and was carrying a cane. How could I have missed that the first time?

"Can you do anything about it?" I asked.

Mother looked puzzled.

"I mean, like ordering a griffin. Or is it like boy or girl? You don't know until it gets here."

"No ordering. Sorry. Have to wait and take your chances."

"When is the new baby going to be here?"

"About the middle of July. A little more than three months," Mother said.

"I can't wait that long," Pat said.

Mother and Daddy laughed. "You'll have to," she said. "This is one thing you can't rush without causing a lot of harm."

Daddy looked very serious. "Have you got that, Pat?" he asked.

I got cold all over. Pat can make things happen, once in a while. Pat looked stubborn.

The long silence got colder and tighter.

"I don't like to do this, son," Daddy said, "but unless I have your promise that you'll do nothing to change the normal course of events, I'll have to fix it so you can't."

Pat began looking Magical. I got even more scared. He's been very self-willed since he was born. Being Magical, he gets his own way a lot more than is good for him.

Daddy shut me out, but I could tell that a battle of sorts was going on—Pat demanding, and Daddy calmly and peacefully refusing to budge a hair.

Suddenly, Pat relaxed and began to smirk. "Oh, all right," he said. "I promise I won't do anything about it."

I stared. He'd given in without a tantrum? What else was going to go wrong? I held my breath.

Daddy's eyebrows met, and he stared at Pat as if he was reading him like a book.

Pat stuck out his tongue at Mike and me. "Anyway, I know what we're going to have, and you don't, and I can promise you I won't tell!" He made an ugly face at us and ran out of the room.

Daddy and Mother looked at each other. Mother sighed. "Now see what you started? They'll never forgive me if I don't produce a griffin. I can't do anything about it!"

Daddy nodded. He came over and hugged her. "Love, we know that. We promise we'll all love you just the same."

Of course we would. But we would also be terribly disappointed.

To Mike and me these three months are as long as three years. Pat's so smugly poisonous that we can't stand him. He goes around looking mysterious. We hope that means Mother's going to have a griffin. But knowing Pat, he could just be doing it to make us mad and keep us from guessing right. I want a girl griffin. Mike wants a boy griffin. We talk about it all the time, if Pat isn't around.

In the daytime, having a griffin in the family seems the greatest thing in the world. But once in a while, at night, I start thinking about what Mother said—horrible monster—and remembering how scared I was when I first saw those pictures of my Uncle Francis. Daddy's six feet tall, and the griffin towered over him, and his beak and talons glittered in the sunlight.

Do I want a griffin in the family?

What Is It?

A STORY BY BRIDGIT O'RILEY

One month after my birthday I found Mrs. Ganshaw in the kitchen feeding Denny when I went downstairs for breakfast.

"Good morning, dear," she greeted me.

She's our next-door neighbor and one of our favorite people. She lives all by herself and isn't busy much, so she's about the only sitter we ever have.

"The baby's coming," she told me. "Your father called me to come over about an hour ago."

That woke me up!

"Come begin on your juice. Then you can pour yourself a bowl of cereal."

"When will we know?" I asked.

Mrs. Ganshaw laughed. "Not for a while yet. About ten o'clock, I imagine."

"Hey!" I suddenly remembered the date. "If she comes today, we'll have the same date. My birthday is the eleventh of June, and hers will be the eleventh of July."

"A one-month-late birthday present? What a nice idea. But don't count on the baby being a girl," she went on. "You know—"

"I know," I interrupted her. "But I'm using the power of positive thinking."

I didn't think I ought to tell her it might be a griffin. Mother says Mrs. Ganshaw has a weak heart and can't stand shocks.

Sounds of quarreling told me the boys were coming downstairs. I got up and poured three bowls of cereal and two juices.

"Mother's gone to the hospital," I shouted over the noise. That stopped them—for a second.

They burst into the kitchen. "Boy, oh, boy!" Mike shouted.

"Girl, oh, girl," I corrected him.

Pat smirked. I could tell he was almost bursting with his secret. He didn't let it out, though. He just sat down and poked the raisins out of the raisin-bread toast. Mrs. Ganshaw soon put an end to *that*.

"Will Daddy come home or call first?" I asked.

"He said he'd call if all went well. I do hope your mother's all right."

The three of us looked at each other. We knew she was.

Mike crossed his fingers—right hand only, of course—and held them where I could see them under the edge of the table.

I crossed mine. We nodded to each other.

I caught a movement out of the corner of my eye. Pat was crossing his fingers, too. I looked over at him.

Inside my head, I could hear Pat's mind-voice.

"Me, too, Bridgie," he ventured. He hadn't mind-talked to me in three whole months! He was actually trying to make up! He was going to stop gloating and being unbearable. He wanted to be friends.

"You, too, Pat," I thought back to him.

He jumped up and ran out the door. I knew it was just because he wanted to tell so much and couldn't.

The other three looked after him as if he'd lost his mind.

"It's OK," I said.

It isn't as if Pat's an ordinary little kid. He's always acted so much older and smarter than his age that you forget he's only four years old, and you treat him as if he were your age. It doesn't always work.

Mrs. Ganshaw was right. At ten minutes after ten the phone rang.

The boys were outside, so I got to the phone first. I don't need to use it if Daddy's calling, but Mrs. Ganshaw would think it funny if I didn't answer.

"It's another boy, Bridgie, but you can still keep hoping."

"Boy," I told Mrs. Ganshaw, who was standing in the doorway to the kitchen. She smiled and closed the door. "Oh, darn," I said to Daddy. "How's Mother?"

"She's fine, dear. Tired and trying to get some sleep, but fine."

By that time, the boys were there. I handed the phone to Mike. He's six, in between Pat and me, and if he were going to develop mind-talk, he'd have it by now. "Boy," I said aloud.

Pat looked as if he was going to be sick. Maybe he'd discovered he could be wrong. Or maybe not. "Daddy said to keep hoping," I told him.

He stared at me with a puzzled look on his face.

"It takes seven hours, if it happens," I reminded him silently.

"Oh!" His funny look went away.

I'd have been positive that the baby was going to be a griffin if I didn't know that Pat can be wrong. He conveniently forgets the times he is. His hunches are not guaranteed, but they are right nine times out of ten instead of just sometimes, like with normal people.

Pat and Mike began to jump up and down.

"What's his name?" Mike shouted in the direction of the phone.

"Sean. Or possibly Francis."

"After Uncle Fran!" I yelled. Now I was almost sure. Almost.

"Right," Daddy agreed.

"Can we call him 'Frankie'?" Mike had stopped jumping. He sounded as if he'd thought it over. "Fran sounds like a girl's name, sort of."

"Good nickname," Daddy said. "But don't ever tell your uncle what you think of his."

We all laughed. As if we'd ever get the chance!

"Keep your fingers crossed. Be good. Don't give Mrs. Ganshaw any trouble. I'll be home for dinner. By then, we'll know."

I counted on my fingers. "Five o'clock."

By five o'clock that afternoon, we'd have a boy-child brother or a boy-griffin brother.

I don't know how we managed to live until five-thirty when the car drove into the driveway.

We rushed out, screaming and yelling.

Daddy got out of the car.

Suddenly, we were all very quiet.

"Pat?" Daddy said. He spoke very solemnly. "Will you ever make that kind of thoughtless, unkind, demeaning promise again?"

I didn't quite understand—especially "demeaning"—but Pat did.

He looked at Daddy. Then he said, very sturdily, "No, Daddy. I promise I will never again take advantage of being Magical in order to be mean to someone. It's awful!"

"And?"

Pat turned to Mike. "I'm sorry," he said.

"Mike?"

Mike looked rebellious. He thought about it. "OK, I forgive you," he said. He didn't sound as if he meant it. But if he said it, he'd stick by it. Mike is a very honorable boy.

"I've already forgiven him," I said.

Daddy nodded. "Very well. Now that we are once again a united family, I will tell you that we have named your new brother . . ."

"Frankie!" we all shouted.

"Right!" Daddy yelled back.

Well, if you think we'd been excited before, you should have seen us then!

"When can we see him?"

"Can we go over after dinner?"

"What does he look like?"

"Sorry, kids. The hospital won't let children visit maternity patients or babies. You'll have to wait until Mother and Frankie come home."

We all groaned. Pat threw himself on the grass and cried. Daddy picked him up and let him sob on his shoulder.

Mrs. Ganshaw stayed for dinner and to put Denny to bed. We didn't have to say anything to each other about not telling her Frankie was a griffin. She'd find out soon enough.

While I was helping clean up after dinner, I sang the happiest song I knew. Mrs. Ganshaw looked at me oddly.

"What's the matter?" I asked.

"I thought you wanted a sister," she said.

"Oh, I do, sometime," I answered. "But it's all right about this one being a boy. Mother says she's going to have six."

"You're a good sport, dear," she approved. "Now, do you think you can finish up here? I'll take Denny up and rock him until he goes to sleep."

"Of course," I answered.

Waiting for Frankie

A STORY BY BRIDGIT O'RILEY

M rs. Ganshaw put Denny to bed and went home. Then Daddy led us into the den. All the lights were out but the nightlight. He'd pulled the movie screen down in front of the fireplace. I looked for the projector, but there wasn't one.

I tried to tell if my idea was right, but Daddy wasn't letting any hints sneak out of his mind.

"Sit over here on the couch with me," he said aloud. "I'm going to break one of your mother's rules."

"I'll bet it's No Magic in the House." Pat giggled. He was getting the same idea I was.

"Shhhhhh," Daddy warned, pretending to be mysterious.

I giggled. But now Pat and I were sure. Mind-seeing. Daddy, Pat, and I can do it directly, like telepathy. The screen was for Mike. Daddy would project so Mike could see, too.

"Boy, oh, boy!" Mike had caught on. He was so excited he couldn't sit still. He bounced and wiggled all over the couch.

Daddy grabbed him and pulled him over to sit beside him. "Quiet, all."

Pat climbed up on Daddy's lap, and I got his other side.

A picture flashed onto the screen: a small, red, wrinkled, black-haired baby boy, not more than a minute old. The baby opened his mouth and yelled—a funny, screechy yell. Loud, too.

"Your new brother," Daddy said. "I guarantee his appearance will improve. If that's the word for it." He said the last very softly, almost as if he were talking to himself. I giggled again.

"I'll show you the change, speeded up."

Little by little the baby looked stranger and stranger. First he hunched up until he lay on his side like a puppy. If you weren't looking for something different, you might not have noticed.

The thing that started people hovering over his crib (we could see Daddy and doctors and nurses rush in and out at superspeed) was his change of color. He got pale gray-blue all over. In another minute, his head began to change shape. His nose got very long and turned hard and shiny. His chin grew and turned into a lower beak. His ears disappeared. From the base of his spine, a tail began to grow—a long, scaly, snake tail with an arrowhead thing on the end. His hands, beginning with the nails, turned into long, sharp claws. His arms changed into the front legs of an eagle. From his shoulder blades, which swelled out into huge lumps, the skin and bones of two long wings began to unfold. His back legs not only changed shape—they'd never straighten fully anymore—but also the nails became claws. His back legs had become the legs of a lion cub. He drew the claws into the pads. His body got rounder and bigger and stronger. All over, his skin grew lumps and bumps. Through them, feathers and fur started to push out.

Daddy speeded up seven hours into about fifteen minutes. Sitting in the hospital crib was a griffin: a two-foot-high, three-foot-long hor-

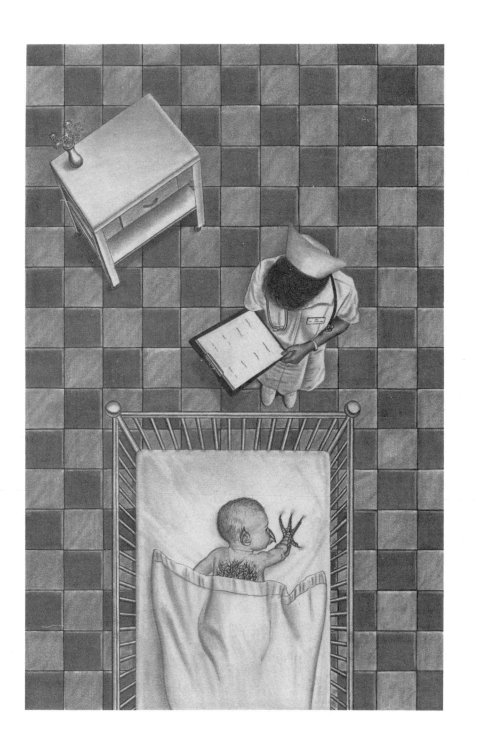

rible monster! Feathers grew on its head, the front part of its body, and its forelegs—striped feathers (I found out later you call it "barred" on a bird—or a griffin). The colors were shades of blue, beginning with a pale blue-white and ending with navy . . . mostly shades of grayish blue. The lion part of him was covered with silky-looking silver-gray fur, spotted both lighter and darker. The snake tail was gray-blue, too, and the spike on the end glistened like new silver. His eyes, beak, and claws were silver, too. Absolutely terrifying.

Pat and Mike and I had stopped laughing.

Daddy slowed the pictures down to normal speed.

The little griffin peeked through the bars of the crib. He said, "Hello."

The nurse in the room was standing against the door, shaking and white with fear, watching Frankie. Her eyes and mouth were open so far that she looked as if she was about to swallow a four-decker sandwich whole. When Frankie spoke, the nurse made a funny sound, shut her eyes, and slowly collapsed like a punctured rubber beachhorse. She ended up in a heap on the floor.

The little terrible monster tipped its head to one side and looked at her. Then he wriggled backward and looked at his crib. He banged the bars a couple of times with his beak, then reached out with it and snapped off the top, then the bottom, of one of the bars. He opened his beak and dropped the bar on the floor, where it made a loud click, clank. He looked through the larger opening, then broke out another bar. Snap. Snap. Clank, click, rattle. He looked down. The floor was a long way away. The snaky tail wriggled around the end-post of the bed and wrapped several times. Slowly, Frankie half-climbed, half-lowered himself out of the crib. He landed in a heap, too, but he rearranged himself and got up. He walked, crawled, and skidded across the slippery tile floor to the lump of nurse.

"Gee," Frankie said.

He looked at her and poked her gently with his beak in a "wake up" sort of way. When she didn't, he crawled over her and pushed against the door.

If it had been the kind of door that shuts and latches, things might've been OK, but it was a swinging door, the kind that opens either way. So Frankie tumbled off the nurse into the hallway outside.

Even that wouldn't have been so bad if the hallway had been empty. But it was late afternoon, the time patients get their medications. A nurse and an orderly, who pushed a cart with the medicines, were almost outside Frankie's door.

The nurse screamed, threw her clipboard into the air, and leaped off down the hall yelling at the top of her lungs. The orderly was a tall, thin black man. He stood there as if he'd grown roots. Then he changed color—as if he were being bleached. His mouth kept opening and closing, but no sound came out.

Frankie looked up at him. "Hello," he said cheerfully. "I'm Frankie."

The orderly gulped and regained his voice. "And I'm leaving," he said. He turned, tiptoed, walked, then ran down the corridor.

Frankie looked around at the empty hall. He didn't want to be left all alone, so he started after the fleeing man.

The orderly came to a cross corridor and turned into it. In a moment, his head peeked around the corner. You could almost see his mind work. He looked around, frantic. At the corner, sitting in its niche in the wall, was a fire extinguisher. The man grabbed it, pulled off the wire, and began to spray in Frankie's direction.

Poor little griffin. He didn't know what it was, so he got a whole faceful of the foam before his Magical fence set itself up. Nothing Real can harm a griffin, so he wasn't in danger, but he didn't understand, and he was scared.

He had an awful time. He didn't really know how to walk yet, and backing down the hallway, tripping over his own tail, slipping and sliding in the foam, was just horrid. He opened his mouth and the most terrifying sound came out. When he got back to the medicine cart, he hid behind it.

The orderly kept coming. He could see he wasn't hitting Frankie, that all the foam was stopping about six inches away and dripping onto the floor, but he kept trying. He pointed the nozzle over the cart to spray some more, but nothing came out. He'd used up all the foam. He shook the tank and tried again. He was paying so much attention to the extinguisher that he wasn't watching where he was going. He stalked Frankie around the cart. Down there in the mess was Frankie's tail.

One step. Another. Trip! Splash! Slide.

"Served him right," Mike said with satisfaction.

The man slid forward on his front until he ran headfirst into the wall. He hadn't been going fast, so he wasn't hurt, but he certainly was surprised.

Frankie peeked around the cart. You could see him decide it was a sort of game. "Hey," he said. "That was fun. What'll we play now?"

The man didn't think it was fun at all. He was still scared of this demonic thing with its long, spiked tail, terrible claws, and sharp, tearing beak.

He stood up slowly.

Frankie pulled his head behind the cart.

As the man walked c-a-r-e-f-u-l-l-y around to the rear of the cart, Frankie slid silently to the back, too—the other way. When they met, Frankie yelled, "Surprise!"

That did it. The orderly grabbed the handle of the cart, turned it toward Frankie, and tried to run him down.

Oh, were we mad!

"Hold it, youngsters," Daddy cautioned. "Try to think and feel the way he does. He's scared and he's angry, but he's very brave. He's trying to protect all the people in the hospital from the monster. Remember, he can't hurt Frankie."

When you looked at it that way, it was funny. Frankie's Magical barrier was up, so the man kept ramming the cart into it. Bottles and pills and cups and glasses sprayed in all directions.

Frankie sat behind his invisible wall and giggled. He did look puzzled by the man's actions. Don't ask me how Frankie can "look" any way. Birds can't. But Frankie does. He has expressions on his face just the way people do.

"Hey," he said. "Why are you trying to hurt me? I don't want to hurt you."

The orderly stopped right in the middle of a shove and stood still. Very cautiously, he peered around the side of the cart.

Frankie looked up at him with his head tilted to the right.

The man backed off. He took a slow step around the side of the cart.

Frankie sat still.

The orderly took another step toward Frankie.

Frankie continued to look at him.

The man stopped. "Oh," he said. There was a very long pause. "Do you bite?"

"What's that?" Frankie looked eager to know.

The man didn't want to give this dangerous-looking thing any ideas it hadn't thought up by itself. "Never mind."

"What does that mean?"

That poor man. This conversation was completely out of hand.

He was saved by the sound of running footsteps. Daddy, closely followed by five or six other people, came running around the corner.

Frankie turned and looked at them. "Daddy!" he yelled.

He started running to Daddy as well as he could. It wasn't very well, of course, because he didn't really know how, and the floor was all slippery.

Daddy picked him up. This is not an easy thing to do, as griffins are not cuddly animals. Besides which, Frankie was growing rapidly and was such a big armful that Daddy staggered. "Hi, son," he said. "You should have waited until I came back. I just went to give your mother the good news. I should think you'd have figured out that griffins are one of a kind here, and everybody is scared stiff of you."

"Gee, Daddy," Frankie said, turning his head around so he could look into Daddy's face. "I guess you're right. But I was lonely."

All this time the crowd around Daddy and Frankie was getting bigger.

From behind the door of the nursery came a moan.

"What did you do to Miss Paulson?" a man shouted at Frankie. He tried to go in the door, which he couldn't, as Miss Paulson's body was blocking the way.

"I just said 'Hello,' " Frankie told him.

"I'll bet," the man muttered. He finally stopped pushing and pulled the door open. The nurse rolled over and opened her eyes.

"It talked," she gasped. "It said 'Hello.' "

"See?" Frankie chirruped.

The man had knelt down and was taking Miss Paulson's pulse. He looked at Frankie as if he'd like to poison him. You couldn't blame him. The minute she heard Frankie's voice, the nurse fainted again.

The orderly was still standing there looking confused. He spoke up. "Hey, ah, whatever you are," he said, "you said you weren't trying to hurt me. How do you feel about us?" He spread his arms out in a gesture that included all the humans in the corridor.

Frankie looked around and grinned. "I think you're great," he said.

"Could I—" a little voice put in—"could I pet him?"

Daddy looked down.

A little girl about Mike's age, wearing a bathrobe and slippers, had come out of her room and somehow had managed to wriggle her way through the crowd of grown-ups. She was reaching up.

Mike got so excited that he jumped right off the couch and ran over to the screen. "Daddy, you said the hospital wouldn't let kids in to see the babies. How come she's there?" He was so jealous that it's a wonder he didn't turn green. I knew exactly how he felt.

"Frankie was put in a private nursery, away from the other babies, when he began to change. Didn't you catch that? The little girl is a patient. I think she just had her tonsils out or some such."

The mind pictures had stopped, and Mike stumped back to the couch. "Oh. Well, I guess it's all right," he said. He didn't mean it. Neither did I.

Daddy started the motion again. The Daddy on the screen knelt down. "Of course, honey. He's a griffin, and his name's Frankie. He feels like silk."

The people were so stunned that they didn't even think to stop her. She reached out and patted Frankie gently.

Frankie and the little girl both giggled and wriggled with pleasure. I was so envious that I *was* green.

One of the doctors leaned over Daddy and touched Frankie on the head—very lightly. "I don't know what you are, but you feel solid and good . . . warm and soft and . . ." he paused, then went on with surprise in his voice, "and real."

He turned to Daddy. "Would you mind if I called in a veterinarian friend of mine? He'd never forgive me if he didn't get a chance to examine—" he patted Frankie's head more firmly and stroked his neck—"this," he finished.

"I wouldn't mind at all. Frankie should be examined before he leaves the hospital. None of the doctors who specialize in humans is going to know anything about griffins," Daddy agreed.

"Thanks. I'll go call now." The man turned away and started down the hall at a half-run.

About twenty people were clustered around Frankie. We could make out some of the things they were saying. Everything from "Isn't it cute? I'd like to take it home" to "Of course it's dangerous. Shoot it!"

Then a funny thing happened. A doctor came down the hall. He had some difficulty getting through the crowd. When he reached the cleared space around Frankie and Daddy and the little girl, he demanded, "What is this child doing out of her room?" He stared right through Frankie. "And what the blazes is going on?"

The little girl looked up at him. "I'm petting Frankie. He's a griffin. He feels good," she said.

The man looked as if he were going to explode. "Clear this corridor. Clean up this mess. Back to work, all of you. This is a hospital, not a children's theater."

Pat whispered, "He can't see Frankie!"

"You'll meet people like that," Daddy warned us. "They cannot believe, so they think you are pretending or are out of your mind. Ignore them. They rarely cause trouble if you don't try to convince them."

I filed that away in my mind.

That doctor must have been a VIP. Two or three of the people in the group rubbed their eyes or shook their heads or blinked quickly several times. Apparently, when the doctor didn't see Frankie, they stopped seeing him, too. People drifted away or rushed off. A nurse picked up the little girl and took her to her room. Somebody helped Miss Paulson up.

At last Daddy and Frankie were alone with the orderly, who grimaced at the awful mess he'd made.

"Bet he wishes he could blame it all on Frankie," Mike chortled.

Daddy-on-the-screen set Frankie down and took out a pocket wand. He extended it, muttered a spell, and made two definite passes with the wand. All the foam went back into the fire extinguisher. The tank flew down the hallway and set itself back in its niche. The cart straightened up. All the pills and liquids and other things put themselves back where they belonged. Even the glasses gathered their shattered pieces and became whole.

The orderly stood there staring. Slowly, he began to believe his eyes. He was past the point of being either angry or frightened. But he was even more confused. Daddy made one more slow gesture with the wand. *Forget,* I thought. *Good idea.*

Daddy put away his wand. He and Frankie walked slowly down the corridor. "Stick close, young son," Daddy directed. "You've caused enough excitement for one day."

The doctor who had gone to call his friend joined Daddy and Frankie as they got to the corner. He gave Daddy a card.

"His name's Marshall," he told Daddy. "He'll be over tomorrow morning at ten to examine . . . this."

"My son, Frankie O'Riley," Daddy introduced, "who is a griffin. I'm Connell O'Riley. I don't think you told me your name."

"Behrenboim," the man responded. "Sheldon Behrenboim." He patted Frankie on the head. "I'll sit in on the exam, if you don't mind."

"I don't mind," Frankie said. "You're nice."

The doctor winced just a little as Frankie spoke. "I can't get used to your being able to talk," he admitted. Then he grinned down and said firmly, "I'm beginning to think you're pretty nice, too."

He shook Daddy's hand and left. Daddy and Frankie went on to Mother's room.

Frankie took one look at Mother and launched himself at her bed. He curled up his lion half and leaned the eagle part against the pillows.

Mother put her arms around him. "For goodness sake, Frankie, what was all the excitement? I have a feeling you were right in the middle of it."

Frankie told Mother, but it didn't seem exactly like what we'd seen. I guess everything is a little different to a person who is inside what's happening.

Mother got angry about the foam and the ramming, but she laughed at the funny parts.

She pushed her hair back from her face. "Guess it's lucky I'm as healthy as a horse. I've got a feeling they're going to send us home tomorrow. We'll see that you're moved in here with me. You certainly don't belong in a nursery or shut up all by your little self, poor lamb."

"Mother," Frankie said suddenly, "I feel . . . well, I don't feel right."

Daddy jumped up and came over to the bed. He started examining Frankie with his hands.

Mother laughed. "Connell, he's hungry."

Daddy relaxed. He laughed, too. "What do we feed a griffin?"

"Not milk or hospital baby food, that's for sure. Find the nearest market and buy a couple of pounds of beef liver, a nice bony hunk of chuck, and a dozen eggs. We'll add other things when we get home."

Daddy kissed Mother and Frankie good-bye, promised to hurry, and left.

Daddy turned off his mind-movies and switched on the light.

We were surprised to see that it was nearly eight o'clock—way past Pat's bedtime. I get to read for a half hour if I'm in bed by eight. I had a couple of books that were supposed to tell about griffins, and I wanted to get at them. So I kissed Daddy and rushed upstairs.

★   ★   ★

I don't think those authors ever saw a griffin in their lives, much less ever met one. What a lot of silly nonsense they write. I put the last book on the bedside table and got out my tablet and pencil.

I wonder if I can possibly wait much longer. I've waited three months, then I've waited another ten hours. How can I live through another day?

Frankie Comes Home

A STORY BY BRIDGIT O'RILEY

M other and Frankie came home this afternoon. We hadn't been sure they would. When the station wagon drove into the drive-way, Mike yelled, and Pat and I came running.

Now, it's one thing to see a picture—even a mind-picture, which is very clear and accurate. It is another thing altogether to see something for real. When Frankie stepped out of the back of the wagon, we three stopped in the middle of our run to the car. We just stared. I could see for myself why people had been scared to death. I was expecting him and looking forward to him, yet there I was shivering like it was Halloween night.

"Gee, he's grown," Mike muttered.

He sure had! His head came just above Daddy's elbow, and he was much bigger in the body than Clement's Great Dane. He saw us and stopped, too.

For the first time, I could feel Frankie's emotions. He was far more scared of us—scared that maybe we wouldn't like him—than we were of him. I just ran as fast as I could and threw my arms around his neck. All the scared was gone, and he was the greatest thing that could happen to anybody. That's what I felt, and he knew it. We belonged to each other from that hug on.

Then Pat and Mike were there, too, and everything sorted itself out very happily. We all hugged Mother. "You'd think I'd been in Siberia for three years," she said, but she hugged us, too.

Daddy carried Mother onto the screened porch and put her down on the swing. I'd put a lot of pillows on it so she'd be comfortable. Mrs. Ganshaw brought Denny down, kissed Mother, and went home. She didn't seem to notice Frankie. We all sat around looking at each other. I don't know who'd have said what first, but nobody said anything because—*flick!*—everything went dark, as if a thick cloud had crossed the sun, but there wasn't a cloud in the sky. We all looked out.

There on our front lawn stood a magnificent steel-blue griffin. He was as tall as two houses. All we could see from the porch was his legs. In a minute, he began to shrink. I kept blinking, but he didn't go away. Little by little, I could see that he had on spats, a red bow tie, a derby hat, and carried a cane. I thought I'd faint.

Mother practically fell off the swing. "Fran! Fran!" she shouted.

Daddy whanged the screen door open and leaped down the whole set of stairs. "Fran!" he yelled.

Frankie squawked like an eagle who'd just spotted an intruder and fell down the steps after Daddy.

They rushed up to the big griffin, who towered over Daddy just as he did in the pictures.

No doubt about it. Mother did have a griffin brother.

Now the funniest thing of all was that I was not one bit scared of him. I don't know why. Maybe I just wasn't scared of griffins anymore.

Mike looked a little green, and even Pat, who's never been scared of anything Magical—even the things anyone with a brain is supposed to be scared of—just stood there with his mouth open.

Daddy and Uncle Fran shook hand and front foot with much enthusiasm. Frankie galloped over and looked up at Uncle Fran. He opened his beak and made some screeching sounds that must have been griffin-talk, because Uncle Fran made some back at him. Then they all came up to the porch. Uncle Fran had to bend down to get in the door, but the porch roof is high, and he could stand up straight once he was inside.

He went over and let Mother hug him. "Hello, Fran, dear," she said. "It's wonderful to see you again."

"And you, Kathie." Uncle Fran's voice sounded a bit muffled, as if he were trying not to cry or something. Then he shook himself, stood up tall, and spoke again. "I nearly gave up on you, Kathleen," he said, trying to sound pompous, "when Dennis wasn't a griffin. I'm glad I decided to keep in touch with the Real World a little longer. As the last griffin in the family who still comes to Real, I have a definite responsibility toward this little fellow. You have done an excellent job."

Mother and Daddy grinned at each other.

"I'm so glad you approve, Fran," Daddy said.

Mother spluttered. "I suppose if you hadn't approved, we'd have had to send him back?"

The three adults looked at each other and laughed. Uncle Fran snorted. "All right, Kathleen, you've made your point."

We had a confused, happy, busy afternoon. The boys and I showed Frankie everything—the house and yard and gardens, the school, the ball field, and all the other places we go. We were so happy that we didn't even notice if other people noticed us.

When we went back for dinner, Uncle Fran was preparing to take off. We walked in on the conversation.

"—and flying, which would be difficult for you to teach him. I consider it essential that he have this training."

"We'd be grateful," Daddy said. "I can give him the general Magic course and considerable advanced work. But I am not a griffin, and he will have to know things I cannot teach him."

"Exactly," said Uncle Fran. He looked over at Frankie. "Now is an excellent time to start. Unless he learns to shrink, he will not be able to come into the house in a week or two."

"Fran, you may have eaten in Magic," Mother interrupted, "but the rest of us are hungry. Why don't you come back after supper?"

So Uncle Fran took off, and we had our first dinner together. Frankie had his before the rest of the family ate, because his food is raw and messy. Even though he eats very neatly—for a raptor—watching him do it can make people feel sick. When he's done, he sits by the table with us. It was funny to have a brand-new baby so grown up. But nice. We don't have to wait like we do with Denny.

Uncle Fran didn't come back until after eight. By this time, Pat was so cross from sleepiness that he was sitting in a corner keeping his mouth shut. Otherwise he'd have been noticed and sent to bed.

"Have you a large space we may use for Frankie's shrinking lessons?" Uncle Fran asked.

"My study, of course, or the backyard. But if you go out—"

"Be sure and stay away from my plantings!" Mother finished.

Uncle Fran nodded. He looked over at me and winked. "The yard, I believe. We'll keep away from your precious gardens, Kathie."

He put a wing around Frankie. "Come along, nephew."

After that wink, the boys and I wanted to come along, too.

Daddy put an end to that. He said, "Bridgit, you and the boys will have to go to bed now. It's past bedtime."

In our family there isn't any point in arguing with Daddy. If you don't do what he tells you, he just waves his wand. Then you find you've already done it and are being punished. He never hurts anyone, but he sure thinks up things you don't want to have happen again. We said good night and went upstairs.

When Mother's not home or not well and Daddy's busy, I try to take their places. I saw that the boys brushed their teeth and washed, and I tucked them into bed. After I checked Denny, I ran to my room.

My bedroom is at the back of the house. I can see into the yard from the French doors that open onto the sundeck.

I grabbed my pj's, turned out the light, and knelt just outside the open doors. At first I couldn't see anything. The backyard looked darker than the rest of the night.

"Oh, of course. Magic."

Uncle Fran had put up tall, Magical walls. He certainly didn't want passing strangers to have automobile accidents or permanent nightmares because they saw two gigantic, impossible creatures looming over our house. And he'd made sure he and Frankie didn't crush Mother's plantings. From outside, he and Frankie would be invisible, and from inside, they'd be kept on the grass.

I said a Counter Spell. The backyard became bright as day—for me.

Uncle Fran was big again, but only about as tall as the ceiling of my room. He was still growing, quite slowly. Frankie was looking up at him, paying careful attention. They were mind-talking in their eagle-scream language.

I couldn't understand what they were saying, and I didn't want to be left out, so I turned myself into a bald eagle and trapped myself in my pajamas. I nearly smothered, and I couldn't understand them any better, so I turned back into me.

Daddy had already taught me how to turn into anything Real and alive, but I certainly couldn't become a griffin. Not even Daddy can turn into anything Magical. It took quite a while, but I worked out a Spell that let me understand what they were saying.

"Remember," Uncle Fran instructed as he continued to grow, "control, *control,* CONTROL! If you don't, you are likely to have one part of you grow faster than the rest. Like this." His beak shot down until it nearly banged Frankie on the head.

Frankie jumped back. He wasn't clumsy anymore, I noticed.

Uncle Fran shrank his beak. Then he grew his tail into a huge thing like a crocodile. One wing got gigantic, the other, tiny. In a flash, he was all right-sized again.

"Uncle Fran," Frankie asked, "how big and how small can we get? Can we get so small we just go away?"

"Good question. No, there are limits. I can become no smaller than a sparrow. At your age, I imagine your smallest size would be about that of a big black beetle. One's largest size is too big to be practical, particularly since we also become stronger."

Uncle Fran began to shrink much faster than he had grown. "There are times," he continued, "when you wish to have one or another part of your body out of proportion. You will learn this later on. For now, we will concentrate on doing the job as it should be done."

Frankie nodded.

"Now, let me see you try it. Shut your eyes, think about growing evenly, and you will find you are doing it."

Obediently, Frankie shut his eyes and began to grow. Not too well.

"Ah-ah," Uncle Fran cautioned. "You are making a normal mistake. You have forgotten the back half. Take a look."

Frankie opened his eyes and looked. He shut his eyes, and the lion-snake parts grew. When he was about ten feet tall, he opened his eyes again and looked at Uncle Fran for approval.

"How's that?"

"Commendable. Very commendable for a first attempt. Now, see if you can shrink to normal evenly."

"OK."

"In emergencies, you can shrink all over suddenly. That is not considered good practice. It looks awkward and untidy. A griffin, Francis," Uncle Fran intoned, "is *never* untidy. We are noted for our cleanliness, neatness, and good grooming. This applies to growing and shrinking as much as to everyday life."

Frankie nodded solemnly. He shut his eyes and began to shrink slowly, all over. When he was his normal size again, he looked up at Uncle Fran triumphantly. "How was that?"

"Excellent! Now . . ."

It seemed they were just going to go on growing and shrinking, so I turned off my griffin-language interpreter and got into bed. I grabbed my tablet and pencil so I could write everything down before I forgot it. Daddy probably knew it, but I guess he didn't mind too much.

I can't wait for tomorrow to get here.

Reporters

A STORY BY BRIDGIT O'RILEY

In the last few days, we've had more visitors than we've ever had before. Besides our friends telling their friends, the *Kenrad Gazette* sent reporters!

The morning after Frankie came home, Mike and I were picking over strawberries for jam when the front doorbell rang for the fifty-leventh time. Mother was about out of her mind. The phone hadn't stopped ringing, either. Poor little Denny was so excited that he got sick.

I knew who was at the door because somebody'd called yesterday about it, though we hadn't expected the reporters until afternoon. It was my turn to answer, so I rinsed the juice off my hands and went to the door.

Two men stood on the front porch, one holding a camera. I said, "Good morning."

The young man said, "Good morning, young lady. May we speak with your mother?"

"Mother had a baby on the eleventh. She's resting. If you want to see Frankie, you'll have to wait. He's having a lesson. I don't think Uncle Fran will mind if you watch—if you don't interrupt. Come in."

I unlocked the screen door and stepped back.

If I hadn't known who they were, of course, I wouldn't have acted this way. A person doesn't invite strangers into her house without at least telling her mother.

"I'm George Rasmussen," the younger man said. He showed me his press card. "This is Sam Peabody, our staff photographer."

"Hello," I said. "I'm Bridgit O'Riley. Please come this way."

I led the way to the back of the house. They followed me to the porch where they could see but be out of the way.

"Where are the griffins?" Mr. Peabody asked. He held up his camera.

"In the yard. Frankie's learning to grow and shrink." I looked, but I didn't see them. "They've probably shrunk down to a very small size. Oh, there they are." I pointed. "In the cherry tree. Lower branch on the right."

The newspapermen looked at each other with "this kid is leading me on" expressions. Then Uncle Fran and Frankie flew down to the middle of the lawn and began to grow. I just barely didn't snicker at the change in the men's expressions.

"Wow!" Mr. Peabody said. He opened the screen door and began taking pictures.

Mr. Rasmussen just looked. And gulped.

Oh, did those griffins show off. Uncle Fran knew when the newsmen showed up, of course, and he had his plans all ready. Crouched head to tail, he and Frankie grew rapidly—and evenly—until they were so big that they took up all the space in our gigantic backyard. I'd seen this before, but the newspapermen were so astounded that they couldn't say anything.

I was very proud to have such good-looking relatives. Uncle Fran looks black until the sun shines on him. Then you can tell that he's a very dark blue. His front and underparts shade to a pale, pearly, blue-gray. He wasn't wearing his spats or the hat today, but he did have on a white collar and a bright red bow tie. Frankie, who'll be the same color as Uncle Fran when he grows up, is pretty in his own way, with his baby bars and spots.

Mr. Peabody took about fifty pictures. He couldn't seem to lower his camera before the griffins did something else he wanted to shoot. About halfway through the lesson, Mike got tired of doing strawberries by himself, so he came out onto the porch. Mr. Peabody sent him to their car for more film.

Finally Uncle Fran and Frankie shrank down to their normal sizes, Uncle Fran about eight feet tall and Frankie about four. Personally, I think Uncle Fran could be comfortable if he were shorter, but he likes to have everyone look up to him. Anyway, they came over to the porch, Uncle Fran opened the door with a swish of his tail, and they came in. Both Mr. Rasmussen and Mr. Peabody backed off as far as they could.

"Good morning, gentlemen," Uncle Fran said. "I am Francis Murphy, and this is my nephew, Francis—Frankie—O'Riley."

"H-h-how do you do?" Mr. Rasmussen said very faintly. He shook himself and took a couple of steps toward Uncle Fran.

Uncle Fran held his right eagle-foot in a hand-shaking way.

Mr. Rasmussen looked at it. With quite an effort, he took it and shook it. Mr. Peabody took another picture.

Uncle Fran sent me for coffee for the men and eggnogs—no sugar—for the griffins. Mike was being very quiet in a corner.

When I got back, I hadn't missed much. Mr. Rasmussen was holding out the microphone to one griffin or the other, tape recording what they said.

Uncle Fran was having a good time. He sipped his drink and said, "These gentlemen do not understand how your parents could have a griffin, Bridgit. Suppose you see if you can explain it to them."

"Mother's family is Magical," I said. I tried to hand Mr. Peabody a cup of coffee. He didn't have a hand free, so I set it on a table. "And griffins are Magical creatures."

Mr. Peabody took the camera away from his face and looked at me. "I don't believe in magic," he said.

I grinned at him. "Then what are you taking pictures of?" I asked.

He let the camera dangle on its strap against his chest, sat down, and gulped the coffee. He and Mr. Rasmussen looked at each other as if I'd just asked, "How long have you been completely crazy?"

I told them how griffins in Magic—the place—could be born to griffins or lions or come from the eggs of Magical eagles or snakes. Then I told them how Frankie had been born a baby boy and had changed into a griffin. I even told them who to get in touch with at the hospital. Boy, was I proud of myself for remembering those names.

I don't think they really heard anything I said. I do know they were trying their best not to believe a word. But Mr. Rasmussen recorded it all.

When I'd finished, the reporter said to Uncle Fran, "Are you sure you're not dangerous?"

"Certainly, we're dangerous!" Uncle Fran was annoyed. "But so are electricity and fire and gravity and any number of so-called natural phenomena that people are only beginning to understand. If you do not handle electricity properly, you will probably get a shock. If you get in the way of my tail and I do not sense you in time, you might get gashed. The difference is that Frankie and I are intelligent beings. We are aware of our potential hazard value and are *intentionally* dangerous only if anyone should attempt to harm a member of our family."

Frankie and I were thinking to each other. I giggled. We were thinking about the man who tried to protect the hospital from the horrible monster and had made such a mess.

Mr. Rasmussen looked at me as if I'd danced a cancan in church during communion. Suddenly he laughed, too. He looked back at Uncle Fran. "Well, that's fair enough."

Uncle Fran nodded.

Mr. Rasmussen looked at Mr. Peabody. "Got enough pictures, Sam?"

Mr. Peabody held up his camera. The back was open. "Ran out of film," he admitted. "Only brought three rolls." He dug into a pocket, pulled them out, and stared at them. "If I've got anything at all. Cameras do not believe in magic."

That statement caused a short pause. I wanted to tell him that Daddy had pictures of Uncle Fran—at the wedding. But that might mean nothing. Daddy is a Real Magician.

The men got up to leave. Mr. Rasmussen was looking at his tape recorder as if it might bite. I could figure that out, all right. Tape recorders do not believe in Magic, either.

After I saw them to the door, I came back to the porch. Uncle Fran was getting ready to return to Magic.

"Is it a good idea to tell the newspapers about you?" I asked. "It's bad enough already. What'd happen if everybody in the United States found out?"

"Credit your father and me with some intelligence, Bridgit. The rumors are all over Kenrad as it is. The newspaper story will counter those rumors with facts. Anyone who is not directly involved with Frankie or me won't remember anything he reads or hears. But those who do meet or see us will remember. That will help them to be less frightened."

I felt relieved.

"Are the pictures good?" Mike asked. He was in quite a few of them—if there were any, which I doubted.

Uncle Fran grinned. "Certainly," he said. "Mr. Peabody is an excellent photographer."

I grinned back. "And you're no snapshooter, yourself," I accused.

Griffins can't blush, but Uncle Fran would have if he were human. "Not too much retouching, Bridgit," he said. "Just here and there. A little artistic verisimilitude."

"Sure, sure," I said.

"Francis." Uncle Fran changed the subject. "Be ready this afternoon at one o'clock precisely."

"I will, Uncle Fran," Frankie promised. "I can't wait!"

"You will have to," Uncle Fran said. He winked at me. "Bridgit, you might tell your brother what waiting is like."

I giggled.

"Must be off." He trotted out into the yard. Without waiting to grow on the ground, he called good-bye and took off, growing in the air when he had risen above the height of the houses and trees.

"Gosh, Frankie," Mike breathed. "What's going to happen at one o'clock?"

"I'm going to have my first flying lesson!" Frankie almost shouted. "Uncle Fran says I can start right away. I'll go tell Mother."

"Mother's lying down," I told him. "The doorbells and phone haven't rung in an hour. Maybe she's getting some sleep."

"OK. I'll tell her at lunch."

That was a magic word, all right. To Mike.

"Hey, Bridgie, when's lunch? I'm starved."

"We have to finish those strawberries, remember?"

Mike groaned. "Oh, Bridgie, do we have to?"

"Yes, we have to. Come on."

We stacked up the cups and glasses and took them with us to the kitchen.

Through the front window, Frankie saw another carload of people drive up and park outside our fence. He rushed out to greet them. I could see where my helper wanted to go, so I grabbed Mike. He struggled for a minute, then said grumpily, "OK. Let's get it over with."

As we picked over the strawberries, we talked about what had happened. When we thought about Mr. Rasmussen's reaction to having to shake hands with Uncle Fran we laughed so hard that we had to wipe our eyes. Considering the strawberry juice we smeared on our faces, I'm glad nobody saw us. They'd have been positive griffins were dangerous.

Lessons

A STORY BY BRIDGIT O'RILEY

This afternoon, Mike and I got our first ride on a griffin. Not on Frankie—on Uncle Fran.

After luncheon Pat and Denny had to take naps even if Pat didn't want to. Mother never forgets he's only four years old. He'd been over at Clement's having his swimming lesson during the morning. The only way we persuaded him to go was to explain that he wouldn't miss anything at home. He found out about the reporters later, and boy, was he mad.

"I'm not tired, Mommy," he insisted. "Honest I'm not."

"All right, dear," Mother agreed. "But come keep me company while I take a nap. I'm lonely."

When I peeked in fifteen minutes later, he was sound asleep on the side of Mother's bed.

By the time Great-grandfather's clock in the hall bonged one, Mike and Frankie and I were sitting on the porch steps, waiting.

As the bong died away, Uncle Fran flew in and landed on the driveway.

"Ready for your lesson, Francis?" he asked, as if he'd never left.

"Golly, yes," Frankie said.

"From here?" I wanted to know.

Uncle Fran looked around as if he were seeing our place for the first time.

Kenrad is a little town named after the first settlers, who came about a hundred years ago. Almost all the buildings are old, but nice. Big old houses, old buildings around the town square, old stores and shops. The settlers planted trees, so almost all the streets are still lined with big elms. All the other elm trees in the Midwest got some sort of disease and died. Kenrad has Daddy to thank for the elms, but we're the only people who know it.

We live in the last house on North Main Street. Our house was on a farm originally. When the town grew this way, the farmer sold all the acreage on one side of our lot. The rest of the farm, about half, Daddy says, is ours. We have elms along the street, three big maples in the front yard, and dozens of fruit and shade trees. The rest of the property has an apple orchard, woods, and lots and lots of gardens. Bushes and flowers grow around the house, and Mother raises vegetables in big beds behind the back lawn. The rest is planted in corn and wheat. Our nearest neighbor farms it with his own, on shares. But no matter how big the lawns are, I couldn't see any place open enough to take flying lessons.

"Intelligent child." Uncle Fran turned and looked down at me with an unblinking eagle stare that made me feel as if I were a bug under a microscope. I should have felt uncomfortable, but he was pleased with me, so I felt six feet tall.

"Where can we go that has less hazards?"

"School playground?" Mike suggested. "It's close. Two blocks that way, six over." He waved. "It's really big, with no trees. The school's new—only one story."

Uncle Fran stared at Mike. "Runs in the family," he muttered.

Mike was so pleased that he blushed.

"Send your mother a thought," Uncle Fran directed Frankie. "Tell her we are going to the playground."

"Can't," Frankie said. He shrugged his shoulders. This is a very funny-looking thing for a griffin to do.

"She doesn't receive," I reminded him.

"I had forgotten that, Bridgit," Uncle Fran admitted. "How that un-Magical sister of mine ever produced a griffin is more than I can understand."

Frankie ran over to the house. He started to call, thought better of it, and went in.

Mike had been staring at Uncle Fran. He burst out, "I wish I could fly!"

Uncle Fran was startled. He swiveled his head around and stared at Mike.

"Could you take us, Uncle Fran?" I ventured, hoping but not really believing.

"I don't see why not," he answered. "If your mother says you may."

Mike and I were so stunned by our good fortune that we just stood there and stared at him. Then we both made a dash for the house. We nearly knocked Frankie down in the doorway.

We pelted into Mother's room.

"Shhhhh!" she greeted us. "Don't wake Pat and Dennis."

"May we go for a ride on Uncle Fran? He said he'd take us," Mike implored in a whisper.

Mother smiled. "I don't see why not. We used to ride Fran and an uncle of ours when we were your age. After all, you can't fall off a griffin."

"Thank you, thank you," we whispered at the top of our lungs.

"Consider this a part of your lesson, Francis," Uncle Fran directed. He grew to about the size of a small private plane, then flipped his tail around so we could use it as a step to climb onto his back. When we were sitting on him as if he were a horse, he looped a circle of tail around each of our middles to hold us on. He has some way of setting the size of the circle so he doesn't squeeze. "Watch carefully. Note how I take off and land. We shall meet you at the schoolyard."

"OK," Frankie agreed.

With his wings held high, Uncle Fran trotted out to the driveway and raced down it. Then he gave a great bound with his lion legs, slapped his huge wings down, and soared off.

"Yiiiiiiii!" Mike yelled, behind me. "This is great!"

I agreed. Flying is the most wonderful feeling in the world.

Uncle Fran chuckled. We could feel it.

He began a climbing spiral, up and up and around and around. It was so wonderful that I didn't even think of looking down. When he leveled off, then began to descend, we were so high that for a minute I couldn't even find Kenrad below. Our house, even the big schoolyard, seemed to have disappeared. Mike and I hung over Uncle Fran's side, watching things get bigger as he glided downward. At the end of the flight, trees and roofs rushed up at us as if we were going to crash.

We didn't, of course. We landed neatly on the school playground. Between us, I guess Mike and I thanked Uncle Fran at least fifty times.

Frankie came over as Uncle Fran helped us off. "Sorry, children," our uncle said. "I have to ask you to leave us now. Frankie and I have to do this alone."

Mike and I looked at each other. Sometimes this is just the way it is. No point in whining about it.

"OK," we said.

"See you at home later," Frankie said.

"Tell your mother I am taking Frankie to Magic for dinner. He'll be starving by the time we're done here," Uncle Fran directed. "I'll have him home by eight o'clock."

"You're going to Magic already?" I asked. Wow! Was I jealous!

Frankie looked as surprised as I felt. "Hey, Uncle Fran," he yelped. "I didn't know I could go until I could fly."

"You'll do well enough by the end of the afternoon. I am a *great* teacher."

We all grinned.

"Now, scat, you two," Uncle Fran ordered.

Mike and I scatted.

When we got home, Timmy Clement was sitting on our front steps. He's Mike's age. He reminded Mike it was time for their swimming lesson, and Mike rushed to get his suit and towel.

Feeling a little left out, I wandered into the house. Mother called me.

"Bridgie, how would you like to go to the library for me?"

"I'd love to," I said. That'd give me something to do. Daddy calls the library my second home. "I'll take Denny in the stroller. Then maybe you can get some sleep."

Mother yawned. "Having a baby is a lot of work," she said. "I feel fine, but I'm so tired I can hardly keep my eyes open. Now, if I could just think of something to do with Pat, I might—"

"Jerry's at Mrs. Ganshaw's," I interrupted. "She said Pat could come over to play." Jerry is Mrs. Ganshaw's grandson.

"Bless her."

Mother handed me a list of books. "Frankie will have to take written tests for his pilot's license. He should start studying."

I gave Mother Uncle Fran's message, gathered up all the books to go back, got Denny and delivered Pat, and strolled down the streets to the library.

When I left the building, I felt very uncomfortable. Mrs. Kranch, the children's librarian, had treated me as if I was someone she wished she didn't know. I was so unsettled that I decided to go down to Daddy's store and talk it over with him.

Daddy's store is called The Practice of Magic, and it's a very interesting place. To people who don't believe in Real Magic, it's an ordinary magic shop with a school for stage magicians upstairs and a small bookstore in one of the downstairs rooms. The Practice of Magic is *not* a joke shop. No snapping gum or exploding cigars or itch powder.

What most people do not know is that The Practice of Magic sells Real Magic. Magicians come to meet with Daddy there and to buy the things he sells. People who want to practice Magic, either Real or stage, can take lessons. If someone wants the help of a Real Magician, Daddy provides it. Of course, they have to believe, and they have to need White Magic. I take most of my lessons at home in Daddy's study because I'm so young, but sometimes I go to the shop if it's more convenient.

When I got there, Daddy mind-said Mother was awake. I phoned to let her know where we were so she wouldn't worry.

Miss Carothers, Daddy's assistant—she's one of the better young White Witches, Daddy says—is crazy about little kids. She ran over, lifted Denny out of the stroller, and took him away.

I went upstairs to Daddy's office. He's usually there if he's not in the store. I knocked.

"Come in, Bridgit."

He was sitting at his desk working on the books, which means he was figuring out the money. He pointed his pencil at an empty chair. "Just a few minutes. Nearly done."

In about ten minutes Daddy closed his ledger, put down the pen, and leaned back in his chair. "What's on your mind?"

"Three or four things," I replied.

"Number one?"

"Mrs. Kranch."

"Children's librarian?"

I nodded. "Isn't there anything I can do? She doesn't like me anymore."

"I'm afraid not. Some people cannot believe. The reality that Magic exists makes them think they're losing their minds."

I thought about it for a while. What an awful feeling that would be. "I guess I wouldn't want to do that to her. Even if she does act as if I'm crazy or telling lies."

"No, I guess you wouldn't. Next?" he went on.

"Well, I started my Apprenticeship in Magic last year. . . ."

"Seventh birthday. As early as permitted."

"You told me that when I passed my first test . . ."

"One month ago. Very commendably, too."

Daddy and I do this kind of talking all the time, usually with our mind-voices. Most people don't understand, so we only do it if we're alone.

". . . I'd be ready to have my first Magical partner."

"True. Someone Magical who's about as far along in studies as you are, to work with you."

"Does it have to be someone *in* or *from* Magic?"

Daddy looked at me for a second. "If I remember correctly," he said (he always does remember correctly), "the rule reads, 'Magical partner.' It doesn't say, 'in or from Magic.' "

"Can I wait a while before I put my name on the list?"

"Certainly. As long as a year, if you wish."

"I don't think it will be that long. He learns fast."

"He?"

"Oh, Daddy! You know. Frankie."

"Do you think he'll want to?"

With some people, you don't have to ask. You know. Frankie would want to. I said so.

"I agree," Daddy said. "You two are much alike."

"You and I are, too."

"True. Nice, isn't it?"

I nodded. It's kind of hard to talk about.

"You may wait until Frankie has progressed as far as you have—three or four months, I estimate. You'll have to remember that he'll be far ahead of you very soon."

"I've thought about that. I don't think I'll mind too much."

"Done."

I catapulted out of the chair and hugged Daddy.

He hugged me, then plunked me back in the chair. "OK, Hurricane Hilda. Question three."

"About Frankie . . ."

"Yes?"

"Well, he goes to Magic with Uncle Fran. . . ."

"And will soon be able to go without help. Fran is a very powerful

Magician, you know. He'll be giving Frankie lessons both in Real and in Magic."

"Do you suppose I could go to Magic sometime? Could Frankie take me?" There. It was out!

"In about ten years, if you both study hard in the meantime."

"Ten years!" I wailed. "I'll be eighteen years old!"

Daddy laughed.

"Why does it take so long?"

"Ten years isn't long. I had to study for fifteen before I was ready to go for my first time—and I didn't start as young as you did."

"Is it because we're human?" I asked.

"Indeed it is. For people like us, mortals who become Magicians, it is the most difficult feat we can achieve. But I want to prepare you, dear. For Magicals like Frankie and Naturals like Pat, it's easy. Pat may never be able to perform the transit alone. But with the slightest help, even unintentional, he could go tomorrow. Of course, he couldn't get back without help. . . ."

"Daddy, that's not fair. I want to go so much."

Daddy shook his head. "We have to live with what we are and make the best of it. Mike doesn't think it's fair to be un-Magical in a Magical family. I don't think it's fair to have been born several thousand years after my time. You and I are alike, and Mike and Mother, and Frankie and Uncle Fran. Denny is more like us now, but he'll end up like Mike and Mother. Pat is the different one. He doesn't think that's fair, either."

I understood what he meant, even if it didn't help much.

Daddy got up. "Does that answer the questions?"

I slid off my chair. "Um-hm."

We started down the steps. I was thinking about the family.

"Daddy?"

"What?"

"Will Denny be the kind of magician who goes on stage?"

"I doubt it. Why?"

"I've always thought one of us should. It'd be fun."

"Don't give up. You've got one more chance."

For a minute, I forgot. "What do you mean?"

"Your mother and I plan on half a dozen children. Wait three or four years, and we'll see if the last one shows signs of wanting to entertain."

I can wait. I've sure had enough of it lately. Anyway, now that we have Frankie, it doesn't matter so much.

And They Breathe Fire, Too

A STORY BY BRIDGIT O'RILEY

Today is Saturday. For the first time in my whole life I wish I'd been born a boy. Frankie shares a room with Mike and Pat. When the boys wake up, Frankie's there to talk to. I love having my pretty room all to myself, but this morning I wish I could be in there with them.

It's six-thirty. Too early to get up. I should try to go back to sleep. But the sun is up, the birds are chattering, a lovely cool breeze is blowing, and everything's so beautiful that I can't stay in bed another minute.

All the time I was dressing and washing and so on, I was trying to plan the day. We had so many things we wanted to do. Frankie, Mike, and I had decided that today would be Pat's day. He missed the reporters and flying on Uncle Fran and was sure to start being unbearable again. I didn't blame him one bit.

I'll admit I didn't exactly try to be silent. I didn't bang anything on purpose, or leave the bathroom door open and sing in the shower, but I didn't tiptoe, either. If they just happened to wake up, it'd be fine with me.

They didn't. Naturally. If I'd wanted to be the only person awake and gone around quiet as a cloud, everyone would have leaped out of bed and asked me what was the matter. Oh, well.

I went downstairs and started breakfast. When the table was set and the teakettle on the burner, I went to the door of the little den—Mother sleeps downstairs after she's had a baby—and peeked in to see if she was awake. She wasn't.

Then I got a Bright Idea. Nothing is noisy about the smell of bacon and coffee, but it can sure wake you up. I started some.

In five minutes, I could hear noises upstairs that meant the boys were getting up. Figuring that coffee wouldn't be very interesting to them, I ran to the foot of the stairs and called up, "I'm fixing breakfast. Cocoa and sweet rolls, too." I rushed back to the kitchen to get the rolls out of the freezer and into the oven.

While I poured milk, I heard the funniest sound coming from the hall. I almost dropped the bottle on the floor. For a second, I couldn't figure out what the sound was. Then I got it—Frankie gliding downstairs "dragging his ta-il behind him." Mentally, I sang the last words to the tune of "Little Bo Peep."

I hurried to hold the door open for him. It'd swing shut on his tail, and that would hurt.

"Hello, Bridgie. I'm starved," he greeted me.

"Hi. C'mon. Your breakfast's ready," I told him.

"What are your plans for the day?" Daddy wanted to know as we all sat down to the table.

"Chores first," Mother began.

All of us groaned.

"Let me do them, Mother," Frankie begged. "'I know that much Magic. Please?"

We pleaded. It did no good. Rule Number One: No Magic in the House. Rule Number Two: No Magic Anywhere without Permission. Our chores had to be done the usual way. Frankie could study for his pilot's test.

Chores are all the same and all dull. We rushed through them, but we did them right. Having to do them over takes too much time. By eight we met in the backyard.

"Now!" Pat said. "Breathe fire, Frankie."

I said, "Please," to Pat, and Mike said, "Can you?" to Frankie at the same time.

Pat said, "Please," and Frankie said, "Sure."

Frankie looked around. "Here?"

Not a good idea.

"And I think I'd better ask Mother," he said. "It's not Magical for me, but I don't think she'd see it that way."

"Ummm. Smart," I agreed. "You've only known her a week, but you've already caught on."

"How about the school playground?" Mike suggested. "Nothing there to burn."

"It's pretty early for kids, too. Coach isn't there till nine," I added.

"We could go the back way," Pat put in, "so nobody'd see Frankie and get scared."

"Good thinking."

"I'll go ask Mother," Mike volunteered. He set off at a run for the back door.

"What else can you do besides grow and shrink and fly?" Pat asked.

"I can't fly very well yet," Frankie said. "Uncle Fran made me promise I wouldn't unless he was here or I was in Magic. I've got a lot of lessons to take before I get good enough to try for my license. You can all come watch next week."

I was promising Pat the next ride on Uncle Fran, all by himself if he wanted, when Mike came pounding up.

"Mother says yes, and only if there's no one there, but we can go, and he can show us."

"Let's go!" Pat yelled.

We ran to the side gate, out into the alley, and along the dusty lane that leads to the end of the block. Mike peeked out for us, checking for cars and people. Then we tore across the street and along the next alleys to the side gate into the school grounds. The custodian had already opened it for the Little Leaguers, thank goodness.

Nobody!

We ran into the middle of the open space and sat down. I grabbed Pat and held him on my lap. He gets so interested in things that he could walk right into the flame without noticing. I didn't *think* he'd be hurt, but I wasn't taking chances.

"Now!" Pat, Mike, and I all said at the same time.

Frankie walked a few steps away from us and took a deep breath. He breathed out a little spurt of flame, like lighting a kitchen match. It got bigger and bigger until it looked like it came out of a flame-thrower. Even sitting back a ways and well off to the side, it was *hot*.

"Boy! That's really something," Mike said.

Frankie ran out of wind and took another breath. "I think I can do something else, too," he puffed.

This time the flame came out as a rope of fire. It got longer and began to wave around. Then the end flipped up and formed a knot around the rest like the loop on a lariat. The whole thing coiled into a hank.

We yelled with excitement.

Whoosh! Frankie threw the loop of flame over the tetherball pole. He reared his head back and tightened the knot. Of course, as soon as he had to take another breath, the flame went away, which was just as well. The pole's metal, but it had become so hot that it had begun to turn red. In that short time! It was great while it lasted.

"Terrific!" Mike yelled.

Pat jumped up and looked at Frankie. "Boy!" he shouted. "Are you *great!*"

Mike and I laughed. It sounded funny to us when Pat said "great," though I don't suppose it would to the rest of the family. Mike and I sure use it enough.

Frankie hadn't any more breath left. He smiled, huffed, and gasped,

"That's all I can do so far. I think I can do a lot of other things, like making pictures and changing the color. Guess I'd better practice in Magic, where I can't burn anything by accident."

Pat nodded in that grown-up way he has sometimes. "How big can you get?" he asked.

"Oh, huge. Want to see me do it? I'm not too good at it yet."

"Yes," Pat said.

So Frankie walked a long way away from us and began to grow.

When he was so tall that we could hardly see his head and his talons were longer than I am tall, he started to shrink, all over, all at once, just as Uncle Fran had taught him.

After that, Frankie got longer and stronger in the middle and took us all for a ride around the playground. He ran and leaped and bounded. Boy! Was that some ride! Finally, puffing like an old-fashioned steam engine, he let us all off on the school steps. It was a good thing. Several boys were coming along the street. Frankie shrank to his normal size.

"Hey," said Mike. He turned to me. "What time is it, Bridgie?"

I looked at the clock over the front door of the school. "A quarter to nine. Gee, it's still early."

"That's what you get for waking up at six-thirty," Frankie said.

"I have to go," Mike blurted. "They'll be practicing for the Little League game. Sometimes, right at the beginning before everybody gets here, they let me play."

Even at six years old, Mike is a great baseball player. Nothing can keep him away from those games. Mother lets him come down to the playground by himself to see them.

"See you later," I agreed. "Be sure to go right home when the game's over."

We all said, "So long," and Mike took off for the other side of the school where they have the dirt baseball fields with the backstops and bleachers.

"What'll we do now?" Pat and Frankie looked at me.

"Let's go home and see if Mother will let us take a picnic to the woods."

"Great!" Pat yelled.

"What're woods, Bridgie?" Frankie said.

"Places where there are lots of trees and bushes and wildflowers and little animals, and sometimes berries. No houses or streets or people."

"I'd like that," Frankie said.

When we got back to the house, Mother had three full lunch sacks and the big thermos ready for us, all packed in a knapsack. It always amazes me how she figures things out without being Magical.

"Thought you'd like a picnic in the woods," she said.

"We were just going to ask." Frankie looked puzzled.

Mother nodded and went on. "Frankie, you can drink out of the stream, but I'd rather Bridgie and Pat drink lemonade."

We nodded.

"Now, about time. Frankie has a built-in time sense, but it hasn't been trained. You'll just have to listen for the town clock. I'd give you my wristwatch, but after last time, I think you'd better let your ears do the job."

Pat and I knew what she meant. Pat fell in the brook, I went in to rescue him, and Mother's watch got full of water. The repairman fixed it, but the dunking hadn't done it any good.

"Four o'clock to start back. At the latest."

"OK."

"Take care. There's nothing dangerous there except coral snakes, and you know what they look like. But if one of you falls or gets hurt, remember—one comes home for help, one stays with the hurt person. Only in a first-class emergency may you send for your father."

This is what she always tells us when we go out for the day. I guess most kids our age don't get to go alone at all. But the woods aren't far, and Daddy can get to us in nothing flat if he has to. Even if she doesn't let us use Magic in the house, Mother doesn't forget Daddy is a Magician.

Pat's Day

A STORY BY BRIDGIT O'RILEY

We walked through the orchard and out the gate into what would be our pasture, if we kept animals.

"Want to ride?" Frankie asked.

I shut the gate as I thought about it. "No, thank you. We'll go along the trail. It's soft and dusty, and it feels great on the feet."

Frankie nodded.

The brown track of the path leads across the pasture to the stepping stones in the wide, shallow brook where Pat always wants to stay and play. It continues up a fairly steep, tall bank on the other side, across another pasture overgrown with all sorts of berry bushes—most of them scratchy—then around the hilltop and down into our woods. It sounds like a long way, but it only takes about a half hour, walking slowly.

When we got to the stream, Pat asked, "Can I wade across, Bridgie?"

"Sure. If you go above the stones, not below. I don't want you falling into that hole again."

We both giggled. Pat hadn't been hurt or even scared, but boy, was he wet! By the time we got him out, so were Mike and I.

Frankie and I went across on the stones. Pat splashed through the water on the upstream side of them.

"Frankie, can I ride now?" Pat asked.

"Sure," Frankie said.

Getting to the woods is pretty. You come around a rock and there it is, suddenly. Because of the hilltop, which is rocky and bushy, you can't see that the woods are tucked into a little valley beyond.

Frankie stopped and looked. "Yes," he said, "I'm going to like woods."

We reached the first big trees and heard the usual chattering overhead.

Frankie looked up. The rest of us have learned not to. Squirrels throw things that get into eyes.

I was ready to tell Frankie this when I realized he was talking to the squirrel. I kept my mouth shut and tried to listen. I could hear, but I couldn't understand. Frankie was sending squirrel language!

That did it! In about three seconds flat, every tree, bush, grass clump, and stone in sight was covered with something alive. There must have been a hundred rabbits and squirrels and field mice and chipmunks and twice as many birds. Even a couple of sleepy old blacksnakes and a toad or two were slithering and hopping toward us.

Pat reached down and started to pick up a baby bunny.

"Stop it!" Frankie ordered. "How would you like to have a giant pick you up without asking?"

Pat stopped.

Frankie listened for a minute. He turned to Pat. "Go pet that rabbit over there." He gestured toward a huge buck who looked as if he could take care of himself. "If they decide you're safe, they might let you touch the baby. But gently!"

Pat squatted nose to nose with the rabbit. He reached out and petted its head and neck and as far as he could reach down its back. He was very gentle.

"They've decided you're safe," Frankie said. "But don't forget and get rough."

"I won't."

If I ever get to Magic, I think it'll be like the next hour or so was. The only difference will be that I'll be able to talk to the animals myself instead of having Frankie translate. I care about animals the way Mike cares about baseball.

Our woods are a kind of Magic Place. I always feel as if I might meet a faun or a dryad or some other Magical creature behind a tree. It's not so big that you can get lost; all you have to do is follow the stream out. But it's really wild, all tangled and dark in places. There are wild grapevines to swing on, trees to climb, sassafras stems to chew, willow trees with twigs to make baskets out of and branches to make into whistles. The brook goes around a rock and spreads out into a deep pool that's wide enough to swim in. But mostly it's shallow, ripply, and clear brown. It's full of crawdads and water spiders and little minnows. Horsetails and rushes grow along the edges. There's a small swampy place with cattails and blackbirds' nests. Frogs hop along the edges, salamanders live under logs, and lizards run along rocks. It's cool in the shade, but the sun splashes through the leaves, making it sparkly. The air smells of water and leaves and mushrooms and growing things. It's nice all year round, but I like it best in summer.

Today, it was perfect. With Frankie along, all the animals knew we were safe, so they weren't scared of us.

"Hold still a sec, Bridgie," Frankie said.

I did. I felt a funny, scrabbly feeling on the top of my head. I froze. "What is it?" I whispered.

Frankie chuckled softly. "She'll come down and show you. She can hold onto your shirt."

Something as soft as a poofy powder puff went swooshing down over my left ear. Little prickery claws clutched into my shoulder, then across my chest. I sort of leaned back and looked down. A chipmunk! She chattered at me.

"Hey, hold your hand under her. Don't let her fall," Frankie warned. "That's what she's saying, so it's OK."

I put my hands up so she could sit on them if she wanted to. She let go of my shirt. I could have stood there a month, just feeling happy. And that was only the beginning.

Pat was in his element, too. He likes snakes and lizards and frogs and other reptiles and amphibians. Snakes are his particular love. He ended up with an unusually friendly blacksnake curled around his neck and shoulders until he had to stoop to go under a branch, and the snake slid off. Snakes are not my favorite creatures, but I don't mind them.

About eleven-thirty, Pat stopped. "Bridgie, I'm hungry," he said.

"We sure had breakfast early," I agreed. "I am, too. Let's go eat on the island."

"Grrreat!" Pat yelled. He ran ahead, ducking branches.

Frankie and I followed him to the stream.

"Island?" Frankie wanted to know as I splashed along in the water. He walked on the path, well back from the edge.

"It's a big, flat rock in the middle of the brook. It's pretty high. You can help Pat up, can't you?"

"Sure," Frankie said.

"He doesn't get to go there unless a big person is along. Even Mike has to have help to get to the top. I just learned how to get there myself this summer."

"Is it *very* wet, getting out to it?" Frankie asked. He grimaced.

"Not from this side," I told him. "You'll see."

"Good," Frankie said. "I guess I could keep dry Magically. I don't think Mother would mind. Wet feathers are awful!" He squirmed inside his skin.

"No need." I pointed. Two flat stones above water level led out to the giant boulder in the middle of the stream. Pat and I would have to wade between the rocks, but the water is shallow on this side. Frankie grew a little so he could step from one stone to the next.

I went across the stream first, Frankie next, and Pat last, with Frankie's tail to hold onto, just in case. After I'd climbed up, Frankie could see where to put Pat. A big bound with his lion back legs, and Frankie joined us.

A whispery-leafed elm leans out from the opposite bank, just enough of it shading the top of the rock so that it's warm, but not too sunny. It's the absolutely perfect place for a picnic. We opened the knapsack.

"The squashy one's mine," Frankie said. He took his lunch bag off to the edge and gulped down the meat. Then he grew his beak down to the water and had a long drink.

"Delicious," he gloated. "Has a real taste to it."

He should have known better. Pat wanted to try it.

Frankie shook his head. "Oh, it's good for me, and for animals like beavers. But I don't think you'd like the flavor of live fish and dead leaves and a certain amount of mud."

Pat decided he wouldn't, so that crisis was over.

I helped out. "Boy! What a great lunch."

It was, too—all our favorites. We stuffed ourselves.

Well, you know what happens when you eat too much out in the sunshine and fresh air after getting up early and exercising. You get sleepy. Pat nodded for a while, then dropped off. Frankie tucked his head under his wing. I pushed our trash back into the knapsack and used it for a pillow.

I woke up all over, all at once, with goose bumps. Right out in the sunspotted shade in the middle of July, I was cold. I was not only freezing, but I was also terrified—and I didn't know why. I lay with my eyes closed, perfectly still, for a minute. Then I got hold of myself and opened my eyes.

I'd turned over on my side in my sleep. When I opened my eyes, I was looking directly at Pat.

He was wide awake, sitting up and watching something in between us. Maybe that was what had wakened me. Perhaps it had touched me as it moved by. A small, slender snake, ringed with red, black, and golden yellow, was coiled in a patch of sunlight. The pointed head with the shining eyes and black, flicking tongue was rising off the ground. He was watching Pat as closely as Pat was watching him.

My stomach turned over.

This was a time it mattered that Pat was only four years old! If we'd been told once, we'd been told five hundred times. We'd looked at pictures in the encyclopedia and stuffed specimens in the museum. We'd had to give the description half a dozen times a summer since we were four years old. But the "we" I was thinking about was Mike and me. Not Pat. As far as he was concerned, here was another of his friends.

No coral snake is a friend of any mammal.

So far, Pat was just looking, not moving. If I spoke, he would probably move. If I mind-talked to him, he wouldn't listen. I could tell he was concentrating too hard. He was trying to talk to the snake the way Frankie had talked to the other animals.

I sneaked a look out of the corner of my eye toward Frankie. He was still asleep.

"Frankie! Frankie! Wake up!" I screamed at him mentally.

Frankie took his head out from under his wing with a soft rustle of feathers.

The snake turned its head toward him.

"Stay still. Don't move," I told Frankie.

"Pretty," said Pat. He stretched out his hand toward the snake.

The snake flicked its attention back to Pat.

Everything was going slow, terribly slow. I *knew* the snake thought it was being attacked. *It would bite!*

Frankie knew. In that split half-second before Pat's hand got quite close enough for the snake to strike, Frankie pounced onto the coral snake with his taloned feet. His strong beak came down, catching the snake behind the head. The edge of one wing pushed Pat's hand aside. The wing stayed between the little boy and certain death.

When Frankie's head came up, the limp snake hung from his bill.

Pat began to cry. He didn't understand any of it. Even if we told him, he wouldn't understand that he could have been the one who'd died.

I tried. "Pat, that was a coral snake. Frankie wasn't awake to talk to him, so he didn't know you were a friend. He was afraid when you moved your hand. He'd have bitten you. Coral snakes are poisonous."

Pat jumped up, tears streaming down his face. "No, he wouldn't bite me!" he screamed. "He was my friend! I was talking to him!"

Frankie set the dead snake down carefully. "Was he answering you?"

"No," Pat admitted. "But I *told* him!"

"Pat," said Frankie, "you weren't getting through to him. He couldn't even hear you. You can't talk to animals the way I can. It's not like being able to mind-talk with Bridgie and Daddy and me."

"I can!" Pat insisted, screaming louder. "I know I can. You don't know anything about it!"

"I do," Frankie said. He meant it.

When Pat gets this way, he's impossible. He goes into a real tantrum and can't think straight at all. He makes things happen, the kind of things you don't want to have happen. Even he doesn't want them to happen—afterward. Daddy's the only one who can handle him. Now I was beginning to panic.

Frankie looked at Pat hard for two seconds. "Pat," he said sternly, "look at me."

"No!" Pat shouted. "You're terrible. You killed my friend. I hate you. You think you're so much because you're a griffin. Well, I'm just as good as you are. I'll show you!"

Frankie put a foot under Pat's chin and forced his head up. Pat screwed his eyes shut. He tried to back away.

I knew how to handle that. When he lifted a foot, I grabbed it and tickled the bottom.

Pat's eyelids flew up, and an expression of gloating triumph flashed onto his face. He disappeared.

"Frankie!" I yelled. "Where'd he go?"

"Magic," Frankie said. He disappeared, too.

I sat in the sunshiny shade and sobbed. Most of my misery was worry, but part of it was envy. It wasn't fair! Pat went to Magic without really caring—just to get away from us and worry us. I wanted to go so much, and it'd take me another ten years!

Would Frankie find Pat? Was he all right? Should I tell Daddy? Should I wait? How long? I didn't know what to do.

In Real time, I don't suppose it was more than ten or fifteen minutes before Pat and Frankie reappeared. Pat was so sound asleep that he curled up in a lump and went right on sleeping.

I stared at Frankie. "What happened?" I whispered.

"My fault," Frankie said. "Uncle Fran got so mad at me he turned white! I was scared and worried and I didn't control my natural Magic. Pat grabbed what he needed and made the transit. If Uncle Fran didn't have a feeler out for anything that has to do with our family, Pat might have been in really awful trouble! As it was, Uncle Fran snatched him before anyone else could and waited for me to show up."

I could tell Frankie hadn't enjoyed what'd happened to him when he did. Uncle Fran pure white with rage was someone I didn't ever want to have to face.

"In Magic, Pat's just a little kid, not powerful at all. The only good thing about it is, he knew it. He was scared blue!"

Frankie looked thoughtful—and a little scared, himself.

"Daddy'd better do something to keep Pat in Real until he's older," he almost whispered.

We looked at each other for quite a while. Not one thing I thought was positive.

I do not want to remember the next few minutes. I got sick and weak and woozy. People do that, sometimes, if they've been as scared as I was. When I stopped shaking and crying and holding onto Frankie, I slid right down into the water and washed my face and hands.

I looked back up on the rock. Frankie was leaning over, keeping an eye on me. "OK now?" he asked. He looked worried.

"Um-hm. I'm sorry."

He reached his tail down for me to hold onto so I could climb up. We looked at Pat.

"Guess we'd better take him home," I ventured.

"I guess so," Frankie agreed. "Uncle Fran helped me fix it so Pat won't remember anything but going to sleep after lunch. He'll sleep it off in an hour or so."

I hoisted Pat onto Frankie's back. That was hard. He's pretty big and heavy for four years old. Being asleep and all limp and unhelpful didn't make it any easier. Once up, he stayed there, of course. You can't fall off a griffin.

"The flattest way is downstream," I told Frankie. "A path runs along the stream. You won't need to get wet."

We started off pretty fast. I don't know why. The danger was over. If there were any more coral snakes, they were probably in a hole somewhere on or near the rock.

"We have to tell Daddy."

"Of course." Frankie was silent for a minute or two. "What about Mother?"

"She'll never let us come here alone again."

"Do you want to?" he asked.

I stood still in the middle of the path and thought about it. "Not to that island. I'll always want to come to the woods."

"We'll tell Daddy first and let him decide if Mother needs to know," Frankie decided.

That seemed to be a good way to get around it.

When we got to the pasture, Mike joined us.

"Got to take Pat home," I told him. "He fell asleep."

"I'm not asleep now," Pat said. "Hi, Mike."

"Climb on," Frankie suggested. "I'll give you a fast ride around the pasture."

"Ride 'em, cowboy!" Mike yelled.

We went whoopin' and hollerin' across the field and up to the fence. It was fun.

All of a sudden I wanted to be alone for a while. "You go on. I'll walk from here," I told them, sliding off.

Pat and Mike looked at me as if I'd lost my mind. Frankie understood.

"OK," he said.

I watched them as Frankie disappeared among the old apple trees. Then I called Daddy and told him—except about how Pat got to Magic and back. That was for Frankie to tell. Daddy said we'd handled the situation very capably, and he was proud of us. He'd check the woods carefully with Frankie one day soon. If they found any coral snakes, he'd move them to where they wouldn't be a danger to people. Also, he'd make sure Pat knew three things: that he couldn't—yet—talk to animals, what coral snakes look like, and how to behave if he saw one.

This certainly was Pat's day. Even if he'll never remember it. . . .

In Charge?

A STORY BY BRIDGIT O'RILEY

Two nights after Frankie's second birthday, Daddy woke me up in the dark. I knew why right away. Babies pick inconvenient times to be born. We'd all been expecting our new brother or sister—or griffin, though that wasn't very likely—any night now. As usual, I'd been hoping like mad for a sister.

"Is she coming?" I asked Daddy.

"Yes, and quickly. I have Mother in the car."

I sat up. "Oh, OK."

Daddy looked worried. "Bridgit, I'm going to have to ask you and Frankie to hold the fort here until tomorrow morning. Mrs. Ganshaw's out of town, and we haven't time to get another sitter."

"Frankie's home?"

"Be here any minute. OK for that long?"

I felt very proud to be left in charge. First time, even though I was ten years old and nearly a Witch. Of course I'd be OK. "We'll be fine, Daddy," I said.

He smiled a little doubtfully, but he couldn't stay to argue. "On the one millionth of a chance that something dire happens, I give you both permission to use Magic in the house. That'll make us all feel safer."

I nodded.

"Now, back to sleep. Everything's set." Daddy kissed me and disappeared.

I couldn't have gone back to sleep right then if he'd passed a Third Order Sleep Spell. I felt so important that I almost wished something dire would happen. Then I thought of what it might be and decided I didn't want it to at all.

I stared out at the moonlight on the porch and wondered what I was going to do. I didn't feel like writing or reading. I wasn't hungry. Going around the house checking brothers wasn't a smart thing to do either. I stayed in bed.

Frankie'd be here soon, and I'd have somebody to talk to.

I don't remember going to sleep, but I must have, because the next thing I knew, I woke up to the sound of Frankie's voice—not mindvoice, real voice. Frankie was standing by my bed, whispering. "Bridgie! Bridgie! Wake up!"

Oh, boy, was I wide awake—and scared!

"Daddy must've left in such a hurry he missed something on the Protection Spells for the study!" he said very softly. "Somebody's in there who shouldn't be."

Daddy'd left us in charge, and something I hadn't even thought about was wrong. Dire emergency was the least I could call it. "Oh, Frankie! What're we going to do?"

"*You* have to do something. It must be an Evil Magician, because he's blocked off my powers. I can't do anything at all!"

If you have to, you have to, and you can't get out of it by being scared, not even when you're shaking so hard that your teeth chatter. "I wonder if I can," I whispered.

"Try something easy—and quick!"

Keep it simple, I told myself. *Something that he mightn't notice because it's ordinary.* I flicked on the bedside light without touching it. Frankie and I nodded at each other. At least the Magician hadn't thought to make me powerless. Maybe he didn't know I was a Witch.

"You're a pretty darned good Witch already," Frankie said, as if he were hearing me think—which he wasn't, because with his powers blocked, he couldn't. "If you can hold him, I can fly into Magic and get Uncle Fran."

I stared. "You can?"

"Lots harder without my powers, but I can do it."

If Frankie could do that, I could sure try to hold onto one Evil Magician for a minute or two. Or three or ten or whatever it took.

Neither of us wanted to call Daddy. We'd been put in charge, and Mother needed him now. Only if we failed would we . . . I put that idea out of my mind, but it was a comfort.

I got out of bed very carefully. My legs were pretending they wouldn't hold me up. First, I opened both French doors all the way, so Frankie could grow and fly at the same time. Then I went to my Magic drawer. I got out my wand and my book and took them over to the bed where I could read under the light. No more Magic until I was ready. Magicians know when Magic is being made. He might not have noticed the tiny flick I made by turning on the light, but a second act of Magic would certainly alert him.

Frankie was watching me so hard that I could almost feel his stare. If what I did worked, he'd know and would leave for Magic instantly.

I almost blew it, but before I thought *Immobility Spell* at the book, I remembered that was Magic, too. By hand, I turned pages carefully until I found it.

I read the Spell three times, beginning to end, paying attention. That's Daddy's rule, even for himself. The end is always how the subject of the Spell can break it, and I hoped, hoped, hoped that the Magician wasn't a great deal more powerful than I. The advantage of surprise was mine, but . . . *Stop worrying. That keeps you from being effective.* Daddy'd said that a million times, more or less. I concentrated.

"You only have to hold until I get there," Frankie whispered. "Uncle Fran'll be here the next second."

That helped. I nodded.

I took a deep breath, pointed my wand at Daddy's study, and *thought* the Spell. One thing about Magic: The more you mean it, the better it works. Oh, boy, did I mean it.

It took.

I couldn't have seen Frankie leave even if I'd been watching. He must have gone at the speed of light.

One half second of stunned surprise was all the advantage I had. The next half of that second the Spell began to writhe and wriggle and struggle. My wand acted like a live snake, twisting and turning and tugging. Wands are one-hand instruments. You break your own Spell if you touch the wand with or to anything. In less than no time, my arm was so tired that I thought it'd break off.

The Magician was trying in every way he knew—and he sure knew a lot of ways—to break my Spell. The words in my mind seemed to want to slip out of place or get lost or change to different ones. I held the Spell's pattern as hard as I held the wand. Shaking all over didn't matter. Hurting didn't matter. Nothing mattered but holding on.

Uncle Fran, a suitable size, thank goodness, appeared beside me. He was so incalculably furious that his fur and feathers and scales shone like polished steel. Angry griffins burn things to a crisp. Furious griffins freeze everything solid. If I hadn't been a Witch, I'd have been an ice statue. A *really* infuriated griffin is the most terrifying thing in Magic or Real. It's even worse than an angry dragon.

He thought the Immobility Spell, and my wand stopped fighting me. I dropped it, collapsed on the floor, and started to cry. I'd never been so happy and relieved in my life, and I'd never been so exhausted.

Uncle Fran wasn't having any trouble with the Spell. He held his cane-wand rock-steady between two talons and had lots of mind left over to mind-talk to me.

"Bridgit, get into bed at once," he instructed. "All is well. Frankie will tell you everything in the morning."

I crawled into bed.

"Tell me!" I demanded the minute I woke up.

"OK, OK," Frankie thought back. "Wait till I wake up."

I was in no mood to wait, but I did—for all of a minute.

"I flew as fast as I could," Frankie began. "Finally I got up enough speed to make the break-over into Magic. The minute I got there, I yelled for Uncle Fran. He didn't even show—just came here. I gulped down some stuff they have to give you back your energy and rushed home as fast as I could. In Real, his Spell over me was still working. When I got here, Uncle Fran called out, 'Don't come in. You are to turn a back somersault. That will break his Spell.' "

A griffin turning a back somersault? I couldn't even imagine how he'd do it!

"I didn't think I could, either," Frankie agreed. "But Uncle Fran said, 'Pull your wings around to the front, sit on your tail, and curl over backward.' I was so mad I tried. Four or five times. Anyway, I managed, and my powers were back. Felt great."

I *could* imagine that.

"I wished myself to Uncle Fran. He looked at me and said, 'Ha! Never know what we can do until we try.' Believe it or not, he made me clean up and get neat before he'd take me to the study."

I giggled a little. Just like him!

"We transported to the study—the lock's keyed to let Uncle Fran in anytime."

Frankie went on in mind-pictures.

There, with his wand upheld, was a huge Wicked Magician, motionless and looking very angry. The instant he saw Uncle Fran he sort of collapsed. Uncle Fran was far more dangerous than the Magician had ever thought of being.

"Good thing he surrendered," Frankie said. "Uncle Fran was so mad he'd have torn that Magician into little pieces with his own beak and claws if he hadn't."

Not a pretty picture, but I couldn't say I minded.

Frankie returned to mind-show.

"Francis," Uncle Fran said, trying to look as if he were bored with the whole thing, "think up something particularly unpleasant to happen to this . . . individual. Breaking and entering, rendering a Magical creature powerless, frightening children, attempting to steal, and disturbing my sleep."

Frankie tried not to gawk. He thought this might be fun. After considering for a minute or two, he said, "For breaking and entering—and making an awful mess—his study should be put in a worse mess. He shouldn't be able to find anything he wants for a week. For planning to steal from Daddy, three of the things he wants least to lose should be gone."

"Excellent," said Uncle Fran. He sent a small hurricane-demon and a poltergeist to the Magician's study with orders to have fun and gather up the things.

"For taking away my power, his should be taken away until he can do a back somersault—and he should find it as hard to do as I did."

"Entirely just." Uncle Fran passed that Spell.

"For frightening children, he should have to do a good deed for a child every Monday for a year—one he can't undo later."

Uncle Fran looked at the clock. "Yes. It is Monday. Very well. And for disturbing my sleep?"

"He should wake up every hour all day every day for a month." Evil Magic is worked at night. Evil Magicians sleep in the daytime.

"Ingenious, fair, and far more lenient than I should have been. Do you want to do the rest of the Spells?"

Frankie did.

After the Evil Magician had been sent back to his totally messy study, Uncle Fran repaired and strengthened the Magical lock and the protective barriers. "I defy *anything* Magical to break through that," he said.

Frankie's beak opened in amazement. All he could do was nod. Nothing would.

Uncle Fran walked Frankie back to his bedroom through the quiet, empty house. They mind-talked so as not to waken the boys or me.

"If I hadn't been asleep, I don't think he could have taken my power away," Frankie said. "We shouldn't have had to send for you."

"Your assumption is correct," Uncle Fran agreed. "But you must not blame yourself. We must begin at once on Signals and Warnings. This must never happen again. Not that I am annoyed with you. You did exactly the correct thing."

"You mean you aren't mad at me for waking you up?"

Uncle Fran chuckled. "Wouldn't have missed it for Magic. Enjoyed it. Not that that Magician will ever know."

Frankie snuggled against Uncle Fran's side.

"I hope you are fully aware of what an astounding job Bridgit did," Uncle Fran said.

"I sure am," Frankie said. "This is the most powerful Evil Magician I've come across in Real."

"Your sister is a most unusual child," Uncle Fran said, almost as if he were talking to himself. "I must get to know her better."

Talk about compliments! I nearly fell over.

In the morning, Daddy told us our new brother, Liam, had arrived with the sun.

Pat's Problem

A STORY BY BRIDGIT O'RILEY

After Mother came home from the hospital with Liam, things were a lot different from the way they'd been after Frankie was born. It'd been so long since Denny was little that the rest of us had forgotten—and Frankie had never known, of course—how much of its mother's time a tiny baby takes. This meant that Mother didn't keep track of Pat as much as she had, and Pat got more and more Magical and harder to understand. Daddy was working with Uncle Fran and was away a lot more than he had been.

Frankie and I had the watchdog duties. We tried to keep Pat out of trouble, and most of the time we did pretty well. Things got easier around Christmas, and we began to think Pat would be all right. But after New Year's we could see he was going to get away from us if something wasn't done. He might even find a way to get to Magic.

We stood it for another month, but by February, we were very, very worried.

"We've got to tell Daddy," Frankie said.

I'd been thinking the same thing. Nobody likes to be a snitch, but this time we'd be telling Daddy something he needed to know, not tattling on our brother.

"I'll ask Daddy for an appointment," I said. "Formally, so he'll know it's important."

Frankie nodded.

Daddy, Frankie, and I met in the study. "Daddy," I asked, "what are you going to do about Pat?"

"We've been trying to keep track of him," Frankie said. "But he's beginning to get away from us. We're really scared we might lose him. Uncle Fran could keep Pat safe in Magic, but he feels it'd be wrong for Pat to go there. He's too young. It'd be too easy for him to end up in Nothing or even in Black Magic if he was feeling ugly when he made the transit."

Daddy slumped into his chair by the fireplace. Frankie fluffed his feathers, and I sat on the floor by the hearth. Daddy threw me a pillow. We watched the fire and listened to the wind. The weather was about as nasty as it can get—and it gets awful in February in Kenrad. I felt as if the wind were trying to blow sleet through the walls. All the rest of us are summer-day children. Pat's a winter-night child. It makes a difference.

Daddy said, "I don't know what I'm going to do. Have you two any suggestions?"

Frankie and I looked at each other.

"We've talked about it a lot after Pat's asleep," I told Daddy. "At first, we thought that maybe if Uncle Fran gave Pat back his memories of going to Magic that time from the woods—" Daddy nodded—"Pat might get scared enough not to go. Then we decided that wouldn't work."

"Either Pat would think he was scared then because he was only four," Frankie said, "or he'd decide somebody was giving him false memories to scare him out of doing what he wanted to. So he'd go."

Daddy sighed. "Fran and I agree," he admitted. "I'm stumped. I can, of course, block off his use of his powers. You two know how that feels. Could Pat take life like that?"

Frankie and I shook our heads. I shuddered.

"If I am forced to, I can—and will—render Pat powerless. It's the last thing I would willingly do to my son—to anyone. Unmaking that Spell is just short of impossible. I think reversing it has been done successfully all of twice.

"Fran said he'd block Pat for me, but if it must be done, I have to do it."

Pat without all the differences that made him special? He wouldn't be Pat anymore, and I didn't know if I'd understand or like the new person he'd be. I felt even worse for Daddy. How terrible to have to cripple someone you loved to keep him from destroying himself. Pat's powers couldn't remain unchecked, but what would he do without them? How awful, awful, awful! We'd never be able to tell Pat what'd been done to him or he might hate Daddy.

"What's been done in the past when someone like Pat showed up?" Frankie asked.

Daddy sighed again. He hauled himself out of his chair and began pacing. "They've either been made powerless or they've wound up in Black Magic," he said. "So far, no one's come up with anything better than blocking off that person's powers."

I was miserable. "Daddy, we *have* to. We can't let Pat go to Black Magic."

He stopped by my knees and looked down at me. "I'm sure every other family who's faced this problem has felt the same way. People who did not do what they must found they'd made a mistake that affected far more than one child, one family."

I'd learned about Naturals gone Black. I was so scared that I crawled over and cuddled up with Frankie.

Daddy sat down again, but on the front of his chair, feet apart, elbows on knees, hands clasped, leaning forward and staring at us. "What would be ideal?"

"Well," Frankie said slowly, "to have Pat give up his powers himself, say until he was old enough to have some sense, to be able to control his temper, to have a stronger sense of right and wrong, and to realize what happens when you choose wrong."

I agreed. "When you and Mother and Uncle Fran thought he was ready, he could have them back, maybe little by little."

"I think that'd do it," Frankie said. "If he wasn't so torn apart inside I think he'd learn to be a person a lot like Mike. And there isn't anybody better."

Daddy smiled for the first time. "There sure isn't," he said. "That's one good kid. Going to grow into a fine man. He makes me proud to be his father."

I saved that up to tell Mike. Sometimes he worries that maybe Daddy doesn't care as much about him as he does about Pat and Frankie and me.

Frankie sighed. "Anybody know how we can get Pat to do it?" he asked softly.

Nobody did.

"I think I'll go to Magic tonight and consult Fran," Daddy said. "You two will be in charge, and the usual rules hold. I'll leave you thoroughly protected, but if something gets out of hand, either or both of you may use Magic—if you use good judgment."

We promised him we would.

That seemed to be that. I got up with my knees stiff. Daddy hugged me, swatted my rear, and shooed us both out. At the door, he said, "Good to know you two are helping. Who knows, maybe you'll solve the puzzle."

I woke up much later knowing Frankie had called me.

"Bridgie, Pat discovered Daddy's away. He got into the study, and now he's gone!"

I sat up straight in bed. "Oh, no! What happened? Is he all right?"

"He seems to be, so far," Frankie sent. "I've heard him calling for ten minutes, but I can't answer. He's too far away. All he says is, 'Frankie, come get me, please come get me.' And he's crying."

Pat, who never cried except when he was furious?

"Meet me in the study," I said.

I put on my warm robe with the hood and reached under the bed for my bunny slippers. Then I was warm enough to think. Daddy gave me the things, and I don't think Mother knows they're Magical.

I rushed silently—another good thing about my slippers—through the cold, dark house. Frankie had the study door open a crack, and I slid in quickly. He'd had time to build up the fire, so we huddled in front of it for a minute.

"Where could Pat have gone?" Frankie asked. "What's he interested in now?"

"Did you ask the Secretary?" I asked. It's a Magical machine that records all events that take place in the study—except thoughts, of course. If Pat hadn't spoken, it wouldn't be much help because the instant he left, the Secretary had shut off.

"It doesn't know. He was here. He left."

Where could *he have gone?* I wondered. One possibility was pretty scary, but we'd better check. "Magic, of course," I said. "Is he there?"

Frankie shook his head.

"Let's see. What's he been reading lately?" Pat's a giant bookworm. He reads as well, as fast, and as much as I do. He goes through one subject at a time—only mysteries, then only electronics texts, and so on.

"The South Pole? Not long ago he read everything in the library on Antarctica."

"I'll try it. Keep thinking," Frankie said.

I didn't remember Pat's starting another craze. He sometimes read Mike's books, though. What had Mike brought home the last time we went to the library?

Frankie said, "No luck" just as I yelped, "The moon!"

Frankie stared at me.

"Mike's reading science fiction," I explained. "He couldn't find anything he hadn't read, so he took out five fact books about the moon."

"I'll bet you're right!" Frankie said. "Here's where I grow. Got to get a lot more power to send that far."

In the study, Frankie could get as big as he needed.

Frankie went to the center of the room and began to grow. So did the room. He beamed out a message. "Pat, Pat, are you on the moon?"

No answer.

Frankie grew more. I could hardly see his head.

"Pat, Pat, are you on the moon?"

This time, we heard Pat answer, "Oh, yes, Frankie." Pat *was* crying, and it wasn't because he was angry. "I've been calling and calling for so long. I'm so tired. I can't get home!"

"Why didn't you tell me where you were?" Frankie was annoyed. "Are you all right?"

"Mostly. I've got Daddy's extra hat and robe on. I can breathe and everything. But I'm so hungry and thirsty and tired. I'm cold, too. Please come get me, Frankie. Please."

"Bridgie and I'll be there as soon as we can," Frankie told him. "Pull the robe up over your head and set the hat spinning on its point. It'll make a homing beacon for me. Can you do that?"

"I think so. I'll try."

We waited a long minute. Then we heard a soft, musical humming like a singing top that doesn't run down; the hat was spinning.

"Frankie?" Pat sent, very, very faintly. "Is it OK if I go to sleep? I'm not sleepy from being cold. I'm just so tired I don't think I can stay awake."

Frankie and I stared at each other.

I had to decide. I know much more about what Magical clothes can do than Frankie does since he never has to wear them. Daddy's robe would prevent Pat from freezing to death. "Probably OK," I said.

"Go to sleep, Pat. We'll find you." Frankie shrank.

"And how are we going to get to the moon?" I asked.

"Let's see how Pat did it," Frankie said.

We rushed over to the Secretary. Now we had a question it might be able to answer.

"Sight-sound review. How did Pat get to the moon?" started it humming. We looked and listened as the Secretary gave us our answer.

Frankie snorted. "That kid is an idiot!"

If anyone outside our family had called Pat an idiot, I'd have hit him, but I agreed with Frankie. Pat had teleported to the moon.

"He thinks he knows so much more than he does. Teleporting to the moon! It's a wonder he's still conscious. Teleportation takes energy, and energy takes fuel. He must have lost twenty pounds! Walking skeleton!"

I knew Frankie was angry because he was so worried. So was I.

"Go get ready," Frankie said. "I'll figure out how we can get there more sensibly."

I rushed down to the kitchen and filled a grocery sack with things that were easy to eat. I also left a note for Mother on the stove in case we weren't back by the time she got up. Then I ran back to the study and got myself ready. I paid attention to what I was doing because if you don't, Magic can backfire on you. But the edges of my eyes and mind showed me that Frankie was changing into one thing after another.

When I was ready, I turned around. Wow! It's a shock to see a two-man spaceship sitting in your father's study. It's really too bad the Space Program doesn't believe in Magic.

"Frankie?" I asked.

"Who else?" he responded. Oh, did he sound pleased with himself. I didn't blame him.

"Where do I get in?"

A door opened in his shining side. The cabin he'd prepared for us was like a tiny den with a couch for Pat and a chair for me.

I sat. "Let's go," I said.

The door closed.

Frankie wasted no time.

In a Real spaceship, getting to the moon will take a long time. We went by a Magical speed that is much faster than light, so we arrived in minutes.

Frankie orbited below the speed of sound so he could home in on Pat's signal. I watched through his eyes as he flew over the mares and mountains of the moon. It was eerie—beautiful, in its own way, but strange and rather scary.

A small, cone-shaped point of brilliant blue light sat at the base of a mountain just inside the moon-shadow.

"That's what I call good navigating!" Frankie sent.

He nosed up in a landing attitude and set down gently beside the small lump that wasn't moon rock: Pat, all curled up in Daddy's second-best robe.

"Go get him, Bridgie," Frankie said. "Don't forget Daddy's hat. That'd throw the first men on the moon, wouldn't it?"

I giggled. It sure would!

I checked my hat, robe, and Spell.

Frankie opened his hatch, and I slid out. Walking on the moon would be hard for ordinary people, but I weighed just enough that I could move easily. I picked up Daddy's hat and held it over the drawn-up hood of the robe. Then I shook Pat gently.

"Wake up, Pat. We're here to get you," I sent.

Pat squeezed his head out. He looked awful!

"That spaceship is Frankie. You can make it that far."

Pat nodded. He needed my help, but we made it. He ate all the way back to the study.

I rushed down to the kitchen, took the note off the stove, and found some more food.

Pat lay in front of the fire. He could hardly sit up. I poked chocolate and raisins and oatmeal cookies into his mouth. He was so weak that I wondered how he could chew and swallow. At last, he shook his head.

"Oh, gee," he said. "I'm so glad to see you."

"We're glad to see you, too," Frankie said. "Alive."

Pat's eyes spilled tears again. "Frankie, I've learned four big lessons," he whispered.

"Think," Frankie said. "Takes less energy."

"Out loud. For the Secretary," Pat insisted.

Frankie and I nodded.

"The lessons are?" Frankie asked.

"Never go if I don't know how to get back. Find the *best* way to do what I want to do, not the first way. Stop doing whatever comes into my head when I'm mad."

"That's three," I said.

The tears poured harder. Pat could hardly get the words out. "Don't do what I know I'm not supposed to do."

Frankie and I stared at each other.

"Did—did you tell Mother?" Pat asked.

"No," I said. "I left a note in case, but I threw it away when I got you more food."

"Think you're going to get away with it," Frankie said, "the way you look?"

Pat shook his head. His tears had stopped, but Pat, who never gave in, was completely defeated.

"No," he whispered. "I'll tell Mother. Daddy, too. I just didn't want her to worry about me."

He meant it! Frankie and I stared at each other again. Maybe Pat was growing up.

"I'll send you to bed, Pat," Frankie said. "Then I'm going to Magic for a big meal and lots of sleep." He turned to me. "Will you be OK on your own?"

I nodded.

"Frankie," Pat said suddenly.

"Um-hm."

"Thank you."

"You're welcome."

What was left of the night was as ordinary and safe as every other windy, sleety February night in our house. I slept until ten o'clock the next morning.

Daddy got back from Magic two days later. It was a good thing. One look at Pat had sent Mike running to Mother. When she saw Pat, she turned white. She knew that scolding him wasn't the right thing to do, so she cleared Mike and Denny out and put Pat on room arrest—nobody in, nobody talks to you, you can't come out. She fed Pat six times a day.

She wouldn't talk about it, and she wouldn't let any of us, either, though she must have known Frankie and I could explain. When Pat started to tell her, she shook her head. "When your father comes home" was all she'd say.

Daddy walked in Saturday morning, took one look at Mother, and asked, "Pat?"

She nodded.

"He's here? He's OK?"

"Yes. Yes and no," she said.

They went into Pat's room and closed the door.

Mike and Frankie and I sat on the porch and tried to keep Denny amused. He wanted to go out and play in the snow. He couldn't understand why we all looked as if we'd lost our last friend. Liam, in the playpen, was the only cheerful member of the family.

I don't suppose it was much more than an hour, but we all felt as if it'd been forever when Daddy finally called, "Family conference. Everybody up here."

Usually we run. Today, we didn't really want to go.

I picked up Liam. We went upstairs, filed in, and sat on Mike's bed.

"Do you want to tell them, Pat, or shall I?" Daddy asked.

Pat sniffed. "I will," he said.

We had to wait for a while until he could.

"This is the way we've got it worked out," he said. "I'm going to give up my powers by myself. All except mind-talk. I can't get along without that."

I nodded. I didn't think he could, either.

"Not for good, just till I get older. Maybe by the time I'm ten I'll have some sense. At least, I hope I will. Anyway, if Mother and Daddy and Uncle Fran think I'm ready, I'll begin to get the powers back, little by little, one at a time. If I don't blow it again, I'll keep on getting them back until I have them all. But it'll take a few years. Maybe more."

The five of us, even Liam, who didn't know what was going on, nodded down-up, down-up, down-up, all at the same time. Pat almost smiled.

"Here's the catch. I know I won't be able to stand it if I remember I had them and that I have to do without them for years." He paused. "But, anyway, if it's OK with you, you won't ever be able to talk about it when I'm around, or even think about it so that I can receive you. Not even after they're all back, unless I've grown up enough that I won't be mad or sorry for myself."

We all said it was OK.

"He'll know he's Magical," Daddy put in, "and that as he grows older and more responsible, he'll become more so. That way, he'll be rewarded for trying hard and getting better."

"That's fair," Mike said.

"Oh, gee!" I sent. "I'm so glad, Pat. We don't want you to be different, really. We want you to go on being you."

Pat swallowed. "Thanks, Bridgie," he mumbled, not looking at me but meaning it.

I swallowed, too. Crying wouldn't help anybody.

It took us a while to get used to Pat's being more like Mike, but it sure made life easier for Frankie and me. For Mother, too. She told me she was very relieved. "I always felt as if I were trying to juggle raw eggs," she said. "One slip, and I'd break something important." I thought about that a lot.

Having a son like Pat must be hard for her, even harder than having Frankie. After all, she grew up with a griffin brother. And Frankie's no Wizard, just a Magical who'll be a Master Magician someday, like Daddy.

I remember what Daddy said about Pat being the different one. Maybe Pat will find out it's kind of nice to be more like the rest of us. It'll sure be nice for us.

Examination Day
Part One

A STORY BY BRIDGIT O'RILEY

"Excellent," Uncle Fran said as Frankie made a beautiful four-point landing, tail coiled neatly over his back, exactly on the four X's Uncle Fran had had me mark on the driveway. "You will take your licensing examinations tomorrow, before you become over-confident. I shall be here at eight o'clock.

"Bridgit," he went on, turning to me and shrinking so I wouldn't get a crick in my neck, "please ask your father and Dr. Marshall to join us. Frankie will have to pass the tests both as a pilot and for the aircraft itself. Dr. Marshall's certification as to Frankie's health will do instead of a mechanic's check. Oh, and please make an eight-thirty appointment at the Grandville airport for us. It's a pity you haven't an airport here in Kenrad."

I said I'd be happy to.

"Good-bye, Frankie. Good-bye, my dear." He bent over, and I kissed him on the nice soft feathers where his beak begins. He took off and flew away.

Frankie and I waved, and Uncle Fran wing-rocked.

Frankie bounced over to the kitchen window. "Mother, did you hear? Uncle Fran says I get to take my tests tomorrow!"

Mother came to the door. "Wonderful, dear," she said. She smoothed the top of his head. "Why don't you go meet Daddy and tell him about it? He should be coming any minute."

"OK," Frankie agreed. "C'mon, Bridgie."

I climbed on.

"Bridgit, call Michael and Patrick as you go by the playground, please. Dinner in twenty minutes."

I agreed, and we loped off.

"I'll sure be glad when I get my license," Frankie said. "Then we can fly instead of run. Maybe my talons will grow. The way they're all worn down, I can't pick up anything smaller than a basketball."

"Hi, Daddy," we yelled as we saw him round the corner ahead. He usually walks on nice days so Mother can use the car.

"Hi, you two," Daddy called back. "What's all the excitement?"

"I get to take my flight tests tomorrow."

"Can you go with us at eight o'clock in the morning?"

"Congratulations! Of course," he said, answering both of us. He put his arm around Frankie's shoulders, and we went down to the schoolyard to call the boys.

As soon as they found out Frankie was going to the Grandville airport tomorrow, both of them wanted to go, too.

"Boys," Daddy said, looking at them sternly. "How many baseball games have you given up, Michael, to help Frankie learn to fly?"

"None," Mike answered. "Why should I? Uncle Fran taught him all about it."

"Patrick," Daddy went on, "just how often have you stayed home after school to hear Frankie's CAB exam questions or to go over lessons with him?"

"I guess I haven't stayed at all," Pat admitted, catching on.

"Most important, how did you act while Frankie was molting and shedding and while he grew his new plumage and fur—when he changed color?"

The boys looked at each other. I knew Pat was thinking how hard it was to get along with Frankie then. Frankie was so surly and cross that you'd have thought he was somebody else.

"Not too well, I guess," Mike admitted. Pat nodded.

"Bridgit was kind and helpful even then—the only times in his life when Frankie can't be Mr. Cheerful. She has spent nearly all her free time helping Frankie, even during summer vacation. She has listened to his memory work, picked him up when he fell, and learned to splice broken flight feathers. . . . You two have played no part in his training. So when Frankie goes to take his licensing exams, Bridgit will go with us. You two will stay at home.

"You may not argue and you may not sulk," he went on in a rather accusatory tone. "She earned the trip."

I felt wonderful and awful at the same time. The boys looked as if they were going to cry. But Daddy had that look on his face, so nobody said anything.

When we got home I called the airport. A Mr. Callahan, one of the examiners, could take us at eight-thirty tomorrow. When I phoned Dr. Marshall's office, you'd have thought I'd invited him to be Most Important Citizen of Kenrad in the Fourth of July parade.

Dinner was a very quiet meal. Frankie and I couldn't think of anything but flying, and we couldn't talk about that without making the boys feel worse. So we just looked at each other and tried not to grin.

The next morning I woke up at seven, checked the outdoor thermometer on my porch, and dug out my wool slacks and sweaters. It was cold out there! Summer was gone for sure. I ran to be the first into the bathroom. By the time I was dry the boys were pounding on the door. I pulled on my bathrobe and ran back to my room to get dressed.

Breakfast was absolutely fabulous, but I was too excited to eat much.

Dr. Marshall arrived, and Mike helped him take off his fur-lined gloves, down jacket, and hat with earflaps.

Daddy grinned. "I can see you're all prepared for a griffin ride," he said.

Dr. Marshall smiled, too. "Well, if it's anything like an open cockpit plane, it'll be cold up there. We're going to have an early winter, I'm afraid. But today's a beautiful day for Frankie to earn his wings, so to speak."

When the back doorbell rang, Frankie went to let Uncle Fran in.

"Good morning, everyone," Uncle Fran greeted us. "Glad you could come with us, Doctor."

"Think I'd have missed it? I'm the only veterinarian in the world who's had a chance to ride a griffin."

Uncle Fran bowed. "Worried at all?"

Dr. Marshall shook his head. "I keep thinking I ought to be, but I'm not. I admit I feel a little silly. It's like being asked to check a full-grown bird before its mother pushes it out of the nest. But I guess a veterinarian is the best authority as to whether a griffin is airworthy."

Uncle Fran gestured toward the yard. "We must get started. It's a twenty-minute flight at the size we'll have to fly."

Uncle Fran and Frankie grew to a reasonable size to carry three people—although Frankie couldn't take passengers yet. Daddy lifted me up onto Uncle Fran, then he and Dr. Marshall climbed on. Everybody yelled good-byes and good lucks as we took off.

The early October day was perfect. The temperature had risen, the sky was sunny and bright with no clouds, and we didn't have to fly so high that it was freezing. Dr. Marshall kept saying things like, "Isn't it quiet?" and "Never felt safer in my life."

When we got close to the airport, Uncle Fran switched himself into the proper radio frequency and called in. He received permission to land. Frankie side-slipped over from his wing position and followed us down.

"Smooth as silk," Dr. Marshall said as we landed gently.

After we got off, Uncle Fran shrank to a reasonable size. "Now, let us go over to the office. Bridgit made an appointment for eight-thirty. We are just in time."

Several men stood at the side of the largest building, staring our way with expressions of disbelief. Not one of them moved a muscle as we walked up to them.

"Good morning," Uncle Fran said. "Can you tell me where to locate Mr. Callahan? We have an appointment at eight-thirty."

One of the men managed to take a step forward. "I'm Callahan," he admitted weakly. "Are you . . ." He swallowed, wiped his forehead, and began again. "Are *you* Francis Murphy?"

"I am."

"By the holy St. Patrick," Mr. Callahan whispered. He crossed himself, shut his eyes, muttered three or four sentences, and opened his eyes. He looked at Uncle Fran and Frankie as if he didn't believe they were still there.

Daddy and Dr. Marshall and I were having a hard time keeping our faces straight.

Uncle Fran looked at me. "Bridgit, my child, do you mean to tell me you did not inform Mr. Callahan that Frankie and I are griffins?"

"Oh, I told the man I talked to," I assured him, "but I don't think he understood. I got the idea he thought griffins were a new kind of small plane."

Uncle Fran nodded. "Quite possible."

Mr. Callahan pulled himself together. "If I hadn't seen you fly in, land, shrink, and walk over here, and if a dozen other people hadn't seen it, too, I would not believe this."

Well, it took some time and a lot of convincing, but Mr. Callahan finally understood that Frankie wanted to take the licensing examinations both as a commercial pilot and as an aircraft. The first part he decided he could handle. The second he wasn't too sure of.

"I am a licensed instructor," Uncle Fran informed him. He produced some papers out of the air. "Here are my credentials." He passed them over. "I can certify that Frankie has had over three hundred hours of solo flight, at least fifty hours of night flight, and fifty more of cross-country flying. Here are the flight logs of our cross-country trips and the other necessary documents." He handed a second sheaf of papers to the examiner.

Mr. Callahan's hand was shaking so hard that he scattered papers all over. Daddy retrieved them, Magically, but most unnoticeably. The examiner gripped the papers in both hands. He took a deep breath, which seemed to steady him a little, and riveted his attention on the documents. I don't think he could really see anything, but he skimmed through the stack quickly. At last he said, "These seem to be in order," and handed them back.

He looked at all of us, his face still showing helpless confusion. "Where do we start?"

"Would you mind starting with me?" Dr. Marshall asked. "I have a number of patients waiting at the hospital. I have to get back."

Daddy took over. He introduced himself and me and Dr. Marshall, explaining that he was a veterinarian and had taken care of Frankie since he was born—not that Frankie had ever had anything wrong with him.

Mr. Callahan shook hands and said, "Veterinarian?"

"If a mechanic checks a plane for airworthiness, I should think the certification of a veterinarian would do for a griffin," Dr. Marshall said.

"That sounds as likely as all the rest of this, I guess."

Dr. Marshall pulled a file folder out of the front of his jacket. "Here is my notarized affidavit of Frankie's state of health and general condition. I have included a statement on the flight characteristics of the falco-leonis-serpentis—otherwise known as the griffin—which may be of help to you."

Mr. Callahan looked grateful that this batch of papers didn't come out of the air. He took them.

"Do you think you will want anything further of me?" the doctor asked.

Mr. Callahan stood perfectly still for what must have been two whole minutes. Then he handed me the papers, grinned, and said, "Yes. Please check his heart rate and breathing. You always listen to a motor before you take a plane up."

He was going to go along with it! We all grinned at each other. The idea that the examiner would be this shaken up had never occurred to me. Stupid, I suppose, but I was so used to Frankie that he never struck me as unusual.

Dr. Marshall took his stethoscope out of his jacket pocket and pushed back the cuff of his glove so he could see his watch. He listened to Frankie's heart.

"A little fast, from excitement, but well within his limits. Strong and steady. Sounds good. Respiration the same." He stepped back. "Extend your wings, young fella. Want to check your flight feathers."

Frankie walked a few feet, turned, and opened his wings. He showed how he'd use them to flap, glide, soar, and land. Mr. Callahan acted just as if Frankie were a plane, and he was checking whatever it is pilots check. When he reached out a hand, Daddy stopped him.

"Please do not put your hands on his feathers. He'll have to re-groom."

Mr. Callahan looked at him for a minute. "Ah, yes. Never touch the flight feathers. I once flew falcons. I'd forgotten that, but I'm beginning to remember. Looks perfect."

Mr. Callahan was going to be OK.

"Now. Landing gear."

Frankie flexed his legs, extended each foot in turn, bounced up and down a couple of times, and showed how he could grip into the tarmac if he had to. Daddy repaired the surface. Mr. Callahan gulped and looked away.

"Seems in good condition," he remarked. "What about fuel consumption, fuel in the tanks?"

"I'm not hungry," Frankie said. "I had two breakfasts before I came."

That stopped things for a moment. Then Mr. Callahan said, "How long can you go on what you ate?"

"Oh, all day, continuous flight, or even longer, at the size we'll be flying," Frankie assured him. "If I were going to get a lot bigger, I'd have to have lunch. But I can eat and fly at the same time, if I have to. Like in-flight refueling."

"I don't doubt that you can," Mr. Callahan muttered. He turned to Dr. Marshall. "Can't think of anything else, Doc," he said.

"Sorry you had to take time off for this," Daddy said, shaking hands with the doctor.

"You couldn't have kept me from coming," Dr. Marshall said. "I've enjoyed every minute of it." He turned to Frankie. "When you get your license, will you take me for a flight? I've become addicted."

"Gee, I'd love to," Frankie said.

The doctor said good-bye and shook hands or feet all around. He gave me a one-armed hug.

"Now, when is the next bus to Kenrad, and where do I get it?" he asked.

"Bus!" Uncle Fran snorted. "Don't be ridiculous. You said you had patients waiting. I can send you back as easily as thinking, if you like."

Dr. Marshall looked startled, then thoughtful. "Well, I've done one unusual thing this morning. One more shouldn't hurt me. Send away."

Uncle Fran waved his cane. Dr. Marshall disappeared.

Mr. Callahan didn't faint, but he did look more than a little startled. He took out his handkerchief and mopped his forehead. "Let's go in the office," he said. "Frankie can start on the written tests. That, at least, I know how to handle."

He pulled some thick forms out of a drawer and handed them across the desk to Frankie. "Can you use that table over there?" he asked.

"Sure," Frankie said. He took the forms in his beak and went over to the table. He pushed the chair out of the way and grew enough that he'd be comfortable sitting on the floor. Then he flipped his tail up, changed the spike into a pen, and started to write.

Mr. Callahan shut his eyes for a minute. "Everybody else out," he said. He opened his eyes and grinned at us.

We wished Frankie good luck and went out.

Mr. Callahan picked up a folder. "Flight Characteristics of Falco-Leonis-Serpentis" was written on the outside.

Examination Day
Part Two

A STORY BY BRIDGIT O'RILEY

Outside the office, we looked for a place to sit down. There wasn't one. Uncle Fran grew his lion part, and we sat on him.

Just as we got settled, one of the men over by the hangar started walking toward us. Uncle Fran chuckled.

"Let us in on it, Fran," Daddy said softly.

"They've been flipping a coin to see which of them would come. This unlucky young man is the loser."

"Hello," said the unlucky young man as he came up to us.

"Hello." We all smiled brightly.

"We've been having an argument," the man said after a pause. "We don't believe this."

Daddy took pity on him. "I don't know why you should. Few people do."

It was right thing to say. We met all the other people at the airport and talked about griffins and airplanes—what Uncle Fran calls "hangar flying." I didn't say anything, but I sure listened a lot. By eleven o'clock the men had decided Uncle Fran was all right—unusual, but OK.

"Wonder if they'll break for lunch," Daddy mused. He looked toward the office door just as it opened.

We got up, and Uncle Fran restructured himself.

"Hi, fella. How'd you do?" Daddy asked Frankie. He went over and stroked Frankie's head.

"Pretty well, I think," Frankie answered. He looked very confident.

"What about an early lunch?" I asked. I was starved.

Over hamburgers at the Airport Lunch, Mr. Callahan asked Uncle Fran how to work the flight test.

"My examiner rode me, of course," Uncle Fran answered.

After he was over the first shock of that idea, Mr. Callahan said, "But in a plane, if a student does something wrong, I can take over the controls. What happens if Frankie gets into trouble?"

"He won't. But I'll fly along so I can transfer you to my back if that will make you feel safer."

"Transfer? How? The way you made the doc disappear?" Mr. Callahan did not seem to like that idea.

"Yes. Like this."

I was sitting on the end stool, eight stools from where I'd been. I'm used to it, so I waited till he switched me back and went on eating.

"No, thanks," Mr. Callahan said. He mopped his forehead with a paper napkin this time. "I guess I'll just take my chances."

He stood up. "Let's get it over with."

Daddy paid our checks, and we went out to the runway while Mr. Callahan got his parachute. Frankie had grown to the size of a small plane and was waiting at the flight line. Mr. Callahan examined him. "Guess you've got enough wingspan for me to feel comfortable. That'll do."

Mr. Callahan and Daddy worked out a way that the examiner could have the instruments he was used to: Daddy borrowed them from a plane downed by a broken strut. He arranged them on the back of Frankie's neck.

"Now, how do I stay on?" Mr. Callahan asked.

" 'You can't fall off a griffin,' " I quoted.

"Young lady, I can fall off a king-sized water bed," he said.

I giggled.

Frankie showed Mr. Callahan how he'd put a loop of tail around his middle.

"It helps him keep his balance if his tail is held forward," I said. "Griffins are a little tail-heavy." I remembered Uncle Fran's often-repeated "Keep your tail *up*."

Mr. Callahan stopped in the act of straddling Frankie's back. "Does he tailspin?" he asked. "Griffin or not, I'm not flying anything that does!"

"I do sometimes, for fun," Frankie said. "It's perfectly safe. But I promise I won't with you. Sit right behind my neck, and everything'll be fine."

Mr. Callahan lowered his leg and settled himself. "OK, fella."

When Frankie had his tail wrapped firmly and comfortably around Mr. Callahan's waist, the examiner said, "All right, taxi down to the end of the runway. Check the wind and do whatever it is you do for a check."

Frankie trotted evenly down to the proper end of the runway, flexed his wings, and said, "Ready."

Since Mr. Callahan had flown hawks, he knew it was difficult for hawks and eagles to take off from level ground. They prefer to dive into flight from a height. Frankie explained that having a lion back part, he could race down the runway, make a big bound with his hind legs, flap his wings down, and be airborne.

Up they went.

They climbed to the right altitude and began the tests. Frankie had no trouble with flying figure eights around two things Mr. Callahan picked out, staying the same distance from them and at the same altitude all the time. Like a figure skater on ice, he soared around the pattern, with one strong flap in the middle.

"Eights around pylons, check," Uncle Fran said.

Eights on *pylons next*, I thought. Those are harder.

Uncle Fran told us Frankie passed. He was listening to what Mr. Callahan was saying to Frankie. Griffins have astounding hearing.

Then Frankie did some nice, smooth lazy eights. He likes them. Next came chandelles, steep, climbing turns. During most of a chandelle, the plane—Frankie, in this case—has one wingtip pointing at the ground.

Uncle Fran chuckled. "Callahan doesn't like those at all. He's flown open cockpit planes, of course. But nothing as open as a griffin."

"Wonder how he's going to like Frankie's stalls and spins?"

We all chuckled. Spins on a griffin are fun—sort of like going down a spiral slide. But when griffins stall, their back ends want to go down first. The passenger has a very funny feeling, hanging there for a minute until the griffin falls off on one wing to get up speed.

But Mr. Callahan was getting used to flying on a griffin. He was pretty good, even if he did yell, "Get your tail *up!*" just like Uncle Fran does, when Frankie stalled out.

"Likes his spin recovery," Uncle Fran commented as Mr. Callahan had Frankie do a second one. "Says it's smoother than a plane."

"What's next?" I asked.

"Spot landings, Bridgit. They're very easy for a griffin. I do hope Francis does not become overconfident."

We waited until Frankie went into the flight pattern.

"He'll touch down then take off again," Uncle Fran said.

Frankie alighted neatly, ran a few steps, and sprang back into the air for another circle of the field. He did it a couple more times. Then he glided in and landed precisely at a line across the runway.

"Very satisfactory," Uncle Fran said. He sounded both pleased and proud. Frankie and rider came loping over to us.

"Well, Mr. Callahan?" asked Uncle Fran, as if he didn't know already.

Mr. Callahan waved his arm at the instruments on Frankie's neck. "We don't need these," he said. "He's better than they are. Greater precision, no lag."

"Fine," Daddy said. He sent them back.

"First class pilot, as far as we've gone. I keep forgetting he's an aircraft, too, even though I'm riding him. We'll have to go back up and check the other flight characteristics." He turned to Frankie. "Or are you tired?"

"Gosh, no, Mr. Callahan," Frankie protested. "This is fun. What do you want me to do?"

"Have to find out about your high speed dives and pullouts. Your stall, takeoff, and landing characteristics are unusual but satisfactory— if you remember to keep your tail up. Then I have to know about speed, power, and fuel consumption."

We all laughed at the funny way he said that.

"Let's see," Daddy began. "Fuel consumption: three meals a day, amount of food dependent upon the size he plans to be. How's that going to look on the report?"

Mr. Callahan guffawed. "Oh, I've got that all figured out. Frankie says he has an optimum size, so I'll give the information about that. Then, somewhere on the back of the paper, upside down, in very small handwriting—number one pencil, of course—possibly in Old Gaelic—I'll mention that he can change."

"Good thought," Daddy said. He chuckled.

"Let's go, Frankie," Mr. Callahan instructed.

As they went to the end of the runway, Frankie began to grow. I was expecting it. Griffins at their optimum size are about as big as the Spruce Goose. Frankie couldn't possibly get that big on the ground at this little airport, but he could begin growing now, then get as big as Mr. Callahan wanted once he was up to altitude. He didn't get anywhere near his optimum. He stopped growing when he was about the size of a World War II fighter plane.

"Doesn't want to break the sound barrier on dives," Daddy explained.

I nodded. The bigger a griffin gets, the stronger he gets, which would mean he'd go faster.

"It's a good thing Mr. Callahan's flown hawks," I thought. "Otherwise, he'd really be in for a shock."

"Very true, Bridgit," Uncle Fran sent. "It's not a normal plane dive—not at all."

Frankie shot his wings well up and back, threw his taloned feet forward, kept his tail high, and dove like a falling meteor. About a thousand feet from the ground he spread his wings and shifted his angle of attack. With a few powerful beats, he sped upward again.

"Callahan's enjoying this," Uncle Fran said approvingly. "He was not in the least apprehensive. He wants Frankie to do it again, larger. Here they come."

The wind was terrific. Uncle Fran put a wing around me to keep me from blowing away. Frankie had been using us as a target!

"Francis!" sent Uncle Fran. "That is enough of that!"

Frankie waggled his wings to show he understood. He went on up.

"Want to go along on a cross-country?" Uncle Fran asked us. "Mr. Callahan has to check Frankie's navigation. Shall we join them?"

I got really excited. When I was flying on him, Uncle Fran had never been as big as Frankie was now. Uncle Fran grew a sort of contour couch. It was very comfortable, particularly as he set up an automatic wind screen, heating, and pressurization.

Uncle Fran cantered to the end of the runway, checked the wind, informed the tower, and took off. He didn't even look around for other aircraft.

That did it! Something that had been itching at the back of my mind all morning finally turned into a thought.

"Uncle Fran! There aren't any other planes around. Did you do something?"

"Of course, Bridgit."

"That's not fair!"

"Bridgit, by controlling the air traffic here, I have merely prevented confusion, nervous prostration, heart attacks, and almost inevitable accidents.

"After Frankie receives his license, he will be believed to be a plane as long as he is airborne—by anyone who does not know better. Prior to this, we have flown invisible to everyone but the family."

"Is that because Frankie's Magical?" I asked. "He has to be licensed for Real, or else only Magicians—and we—can see him?"

Uncle Fran nodded. "However, once he lands, he can be seen as himself by anyone who believes in Magic."

Mr. Callahan handed Frankie a map and pointed to where he wanted Frankie to go.

"In a small plane, it's a four-hour trip to Loring, if we scout around a bit. Then, half that time back, crow flight. At this size, I should think you could make the whole trip by five o'clock, right?"

Frankie nodded.

"OK. Go over the racetrack, Lake Williams, the new freeway, pass Paddon Heights on the left, Enderby on the right, and bisect Hempstead," Mr. Callahan directed. "Then straight back. That should give me a good sample."

Frankie handed the map back. "OK, I've memorized it."

This time, Uncle Fran flew wing on Frankie. Off we sped.

In a very short time we had shot over the first checkpoint dead center. Frankie turned north and set off for Lake Williams.

We saw Mr. Callahan lean forward to talk to Frankie. It isn't necessary, but we do the same thing. Frankie cut us in on the conversation.

"Altitude and attitude are inborn characteristics, right? Is direction the same?"

"Right. Once I learned a name for certain feelings about the way I was facing, I never had to worry about it again. Can't go wrong, even in the dark."

"Handy." Mr. Callahan leaned back and stretched out. "You know, Frankie, griffin-flying could make a very lazy pilot of me. I never flew alone before without having to keep half an eye on the instruments or controls, or at least look around for what else is in the sky."

"That's instinctive in griffins," Frankie said. "I know the location of everything in the sky larger than a gnat. Clouds and weather fronts, too."

"There go the meteorologists and the auto-pilot manufacturers." Mr. Callahan chuckled.

Frankie snorted. "Hardly. Uncle Fran and I are the only two griffins in Real."

We flew for another few minutes. Then Frankie said, "Lake Williams ahead."

We looked. There it was, shining in the sunlight.

"Sure can't beat that for navigating," the instructor noted.

We made the schedule perfectly. At five o'clock on the dot we touched down at the Grandville airport. Mr. Callahan jumped off Frankie's tail-step and came over to us.

"As far as I'm concerned, the airplane industry can go bust tomorrow," he remarked as he came up, "if you'll invite a few million griffins to take over. I'll choose one every time.

"Frankie will get his licenses," he finished. "When you get over here again, look me up."

We all smiled at each other.

When we'd shaken hands and said thank you, Mr. Callahan stepped back, and we took off for home.

Frankie and I were tired that night, and we were excused from all chores. Frankie says he doesn't get tired flying, but he confessed he thought his wings were going to fall off by the time we got home. I don't know why I'm so tired. I haven't done anything special. Mother says it was the excitement.

First Flight on Frankie

A STORY BY BRIDGIT O'RILEY

We met the mailman every day for three weeks, and Frankie's licenses didn't come. Yesterday, we got so worried that we tried to get Daddy to call the CAB offices. He told us to be patient. We began to think that Frankie hadn't passed, or they wouldn't license griffins anymore, though of course we didn't say so out loud. Oh, were we miserable.

Yesterday morning we met the mailman as usual. He handed us a batch of uninteresting stuff for Mother and Daddy.

"Sorry I can't give you that special letter," he said.

It wasn't his fault, but we'd begun to dislike him anyway.

About noon it began to rain. We wandered around snapping at each other until Mother got us together on the back porch to play Monopoly.

Quite a while later, the front doorbell rang. We looked at each other. Nobody wanted to go.

Finally Frankie said, "OK, OK, I'll go."

Not more than a minute later he exploded through the door onto the porch.

"It came!" he shouted. "By registered mail. I had to sign for it!" He held out an envelope. "Here it is!"

We scattered Monopoly money, cards, and pieces all over in our rush to see. Mother dropped the envelope twice before she could get it open. She spread out the papers on the table so we could all look at them at the same time.

Frankie's commercial pilot's license and his certification as an aircraft. He had numbers and everything!

"Let's go flying right now," Mike yelled. He rushed out of the room and started upstairs. Daddy was so proud of the boys for behaving well about not going with us when Frankie took his tests that he'd given both of the older ones pilot's helmets.

"Michael!" Mother called. "Come down here. I am truly sorry, but you are not going flying for the first time in this rain. Frankie will get wet feathers, and that makes flying difficult. You'll have to wait until the rain stops. We'll all keep our fingers crossed for good weather."

All of us begged and begged. Frankie told Mother he could keep us dry Magically, but she meant what she said. We had to be content with picking up the Monopoly game and sitting around the table over a map planning the trips we'd take the next day.

When Daddy got home we practically knocked him down to show him the licenses.

"Can we go tomorrow?" the boys yelled.

Daddy put his hands over his ears. "If it isn't rainy or foggy," he shouted back.

We giggled and quieted down.

"First thing?" Mike wanted to know.

"Right after church," Daddy agreed.

"Can we go to early Mass?" Pat asked.

All of us shouted. Pat is the most difficult child to get out of bed you ever met in your life.

"Patrick," Mother said, "if you are up, washed, dressed, and all ready to go by a quarter of seven, we will go to early Mass. It's up to you."

"I'll be ready," Pat promised. "Bridgie, can I borrow your alarm clock?"

Pat got us all up at six o'clock this morning. He'd already taken a bath and dressed! "I'll feed Liam, Mother," he said. "You go get ready."

Mother stared at him. She handed him the spoon and left the room, putting on a good imitation of somebody who'd been hypnotized. We all spluttered. Liam doesn't like the kind of cereal Pat fed him, but he ate it very neatly.

We made early Mass on time. Father Maloney gaped as he saw us all troop in. Mother, Mike, and Dennis often go to early Mass, but Daddy, Pat, and I go to eleven o'clock most Sundays.

I tried to pay attention, but I know I didn't. God understood. I hoped.

We went outside with our fingers crossed. The morning had been a little gray but not foggy, and there hadn't been any rain. Had things cleared up enough that Daddy'd let us go?

Lovely sunshine! We cheered.

When everyone had left the parking lot, the boys got on Frankie. We'd agreed that they could have the first ride all to themselves because they'd been so good. I wasn't all that happy about it, but I tried to act as if I didn't mind. I'd get to ride soon—and probably a lot more than they ever would—so who was I to be a selfish pig? I told myself that, but it didn't make me feel much better. Mother squeezed my shoulder. She understood, and that helped a little.

Frankie checked the wind and trotted over so he'd have a good long run.

"What a beautiful takeoff," Mother murmured as they soared into the sky.

When we got home we had barely had time to change our clothes before Frankie brought the boys in for a perfect landing on the driveway. As they tumbled off and ran into the house, they almost ran into Mrs. Ganshaw.

"Thought I'd come over and get Liam. I'll take care of him for you today, Kathie. My treat."

Mother hugged her.

Mrs. Ganshaw beamed. "We'll wait here on the porch and watch you take off." She had accepted Frankie as if she expected her next-door neighbor to be a griffin.

The boys changed, Mother threw the makings for a lunch into the big picnic basket, and I got Liam's diapers and things and took them next door.

"Come on, family. Let's go," Daddy said as we all assembled in the front hall.

Daddy locked the door while Mother kissed Liam good-bye.

"Come back as late as you like, Kathie," Mrs. Ganshaw said. "If it's after Liam's bedtime, just leave him overnight. He's good as gold. Have a lovely time."

We all climbed on Frankie. Mother got on first, with Denny in front of her so she could hold onto him, then Pat and me and Mike and Daddy. Frankie had to grow his middle a little, but that wouldn't affect his flying.

Wow! What a takeoff! Frankie was showing off. We went practically straight up!

Kenrad is so little that Frankie was away from the whole town in a couple of minutes. He circled so we could look down.

"That's the place we had the great picnic last year," Daddy said, pointing.

"There's the new highway," Mike shouted, pointing the other way.

"Is that Wrightson's farm?" Pat asked. Jimmy Wrightson is in his class at school.

"I think so," Mother said. "It's hard to tell from the air."

"Right," Daddy confirmed. "It's on the road to my parents' house."

"Let's go see them!" I suggested.

Mother grinned. "Nope. Let's go see Peggy and Jack."

We all whooped. Aunt Peggy and Uncle Jack are our favorite relatives. They live on a farm about twenty-five miles from Kenrad. Aunt Peggy is Mother's youngest sister. She only got married two years ago. The boys like her, too, and they're nuts about Uncle Jack. He takes us fishing and bobsledding and all sorts of things.

"Peggy and Jack's it is," Daddy agreed.

Frankie sped.

"What's all the pop-pop-pop?" Denny asked.

"What do you mean, son?" Daddy asked him.

"Listen. Down there. Pop-pop-pop."

Everybody leaned over to listen.

Daddy straightened up. "I forgot. Hunting season started early this year. Yesterday was the opening day. We're safe on Frankie, and we'll be all right when we get off at the farm. It's posted."

"What does that mean?" Denny asked.

"Uncle Jack puts up notices all around his farm. No hunting."

"But he hunts," Mike protested.

"Only on his own land, for food, and only when the county says there are too many deer or whatever to live through the winter."

We landed safely in the farmyard and went running up to the house.

Mother knocked her special knock and opened the door. "Peggy? Hey, Peggy! Where are you?"

A funny voice called, "Oh, Kathie! I'm in bed. Don't come up! I've got the flu."

I couldn't decide whether Aunt Peggy had just been crying or whether she was about to start. Maybe both.

Mother went halfway up the stairs. "Where's Jack?"

Now I knew Aunt Peggy was crying. "Oh, Kathie! Everything is awful! He's nearly as sick as I am, but he had to go out and paint COW on all our stock so the hunters wouldn't shoot them. We had three cows killed last year. The hunters actually came over on our land and tried to pull one of them away. Jack caught them at it and called the sheriff. But to make matters worse, Heilbron broke out of the barn. If Jack doesn't find him, he'll probably get shot. And there goes all that money, and our new herd, and—and Ernie's on his day off—Jack said he could go—and—" Aunt Peggy broke down altogether.

"Who's Heilbron?" Denny asked.

"Uncle Jack's new herd bull," Daddy told him. "Cost a lot of money. Not a good animal to meet up with, either. If a hunter shot him, he could say he was being attacked."

"I'll find him, Daddy," Frankie said. "C'mon, Bridgie, you can help me look."

"Right," Daddy said. "Mike, Pat, you get out there and finish painting the cattle. Tell Uncle Jack to come in. We'll take over." He leaped up the stairs two at a time, glowing blue-green.

Mother stared at him as he went by. He stopped long enough to say, "I don't want to get the flu—or to be a carrier. Take Denny out on the porch, Kathie. I'll clean things up in here when I've done what I can for Peggy."

I pounded out after Frankie as Mother picked up the phone.

Calling the doctor, I guess, I thought. *Too bad it's Sunday.*

Frankie and I took off. He kept low so we could look for Heilbron, and some of the bullets came pretty close. After all, it was deer season. A lot of first-time hunters must have been in the area.

"Can you see if he went through the fence?" Frankie asked, swerving away from another wild shot. I wondered if we were being shot at intentionally—and if so, what the hunters thought we were.

"Ah-ha!" I pointed. "Over there. Turn to the right a little. See?" Heilbron's tracks and the big hole he'd made in the fence were easy to spot.

Frankie flew over, turned along the path the bull had made, and winged slowly along.

Heilbron had taken off into the wooded lot that runs down to the scrub along the little river. He could be anywhere by now and well hidden. The woods were dense. The trees hadn't lost all their leaves, and quite a few evergreens grew in with the hardwoods.

"Why don't you call him?" I asked.

"I did. If he heard—and understood—he didn't answer."

"Oh."

"Not very smart, cattle," Frankie explained.

I hoped that was all it was. Heilbron could be hiding from us as much as he was hiding from the hunters. I hoped he was hiding from them. He could also be dead, but I didn't want to believe that, so I tried not to think it.

We made short, tight passes over the whole area. Could he possibly have come this far?

"Got him!" Frankie said. "Some idiot did shoot him, but he wasn't hurt all that much, and he got away. I guess Uncle Jack's lucky the hunter didn't want to follow him down into the scrub. Maybe he didn't even know he'd hit him."

"A bull's a pretty big target," I said.

I was completely disgusted. Feeling the way I do about animals, I've never wanted to hunt, but Daddy and Uncle Jack and a lot of my uncles and cousins do, even some of the girls. We all eat venison and dove and duck. I couldn't at first, until Daddy explained. "There's only so much natural food, Bridgie," he said. If the herds are too big, they run out of food. Deer invade orchards and kill young trees. Many of them starve to death.

"A good hunter hunts only for food. He takes only the legal limit. He kills quick and clean, and the animal doesn't suffer. Isn't that better? If you were a deer, which would you rather have happen to you?"

"But, Daddy," I remember asking, "what if the hunter only wounds the animal? It'll bleed to death, or worse!"

"No hunter who does not follow and kill a wounded quarry should ever be allowed to go into the field," he said. "I get very angry about them and about poachers—people who hunt out of season." He also swears under his breath at trophy hunters—people who kill something so they can hang its head on the wall to show what great hunters they are.

Frankie hovered. "He's right below us, Bridgie. Can you see him?"

I could, and I was worried. Heilbron was lying down, and it wasn't because he was taking a rest to chew his cud. He was hurt. "Um-hm. How are we going to get him back to the farm?"

"Hold on, Bridgie. I'm going to grow. I'll get big enough that I can wrap my tail around him four or five times and lift him up. I can carry him back."

I tucked my feet up, and Frankie grew. He had to climb a little so he wouldn't squash things below him. When he was big enough, his tail got longer and thicker and sort of padded and snaked off into the brush below.

Heilbron tried to get up and run away. Oh, was he scared! Frankie explained over and over what we were going to do, but that bull must have a head of solid bone.

At last, Frankie managed to get a good hold. Up we went, slowly, swinging the big body of the bellowing animal clear of the treetops. I looked down. All the shooting had stopped.

"Did you do something?" I asked Frankie.

"No," he sent. "But I'll bet those men have a hunting story nobody'll believe."

By the time we were back, Mother and Denny were cooking chicken soup for Aunt Peggy and Uncle Jack, who were both in bed. Pat and Mike had finished painting COW in big orange letters on all the animals and were hard at work on the farm chores. Daddy had finished chasing all the germs out of the house and was repairing Heilbron's big box stall. When Frankie called him, Daddy came out and directed the placing of the wounded bull.

Frankie shrank and landed, and we both rushed into the barn.

"We need a vet," Daddy said. "I can staunch the bleeding and probably eliminate most of the infection, but I'm no expert on bull anatomy. If I tried to get the bullets out, I might hurt him worse.

"Bridgie, call Dr. Marshall and explain. Frankie, go get him. Don't take no for an answer, either of you."

Dr. Marshall was in, thank heavens. At this time of year, he's often out, doing exactly what he'd have to do here—trying to save the life of some farm animal shot by a hunter with a heavy trigger finger, terrible eyesight, and too much desire to kill something. I ran out and signaled Frankie. "He's home."

Frankie sprang into the air.

Mother rushed onto the porch, shouting, "Stop at the drugstore! The doctor telephoned in a prescription for Peggy and Jack."

Frankie wing-rocked and sped off.

We didn't get home until about midnight. Aunt Peggy and Uncle Jack were in bed getting over the flu. Heilbron was out of danger. Frankie had flown Dr. Marshall home. All the stock had been fed and watered. Mother wanted to stay and take care of everything, but Daddy wouldn't let her. The hired man, Ernie, would be back the next morning. He was a good farmer and a good man, and he would take care of Aunt Peggy and Uncle Jack.

"Good thing you got your license," I said to Frankie as we went up to bed.

Frankie yawned. "Right. But I didn't think I'd use it this way the first day."

None of us had.

Carnival Rides

A STORY BY BRIDGIT O'RILEY

"That's terrible! What're we going to do?"

The Halloween carnival would begin in an hour, and the company that brings in the rides had just called Mother. They'd had a breakdown and wouldn't be there at all!

"It'll ruin it! All the kids've saved up for weeks. Just the booths the PTA does for the little kids won't be enough!"

The Halloween carnival is about the biggest thing that happens in Kenrad—except the Fourth of July. Everybody in the county goes in costume—even our whole police force, all six of the officers, in uniforms about fifty years old that somebody found in the station attic.

Now the carnival would be ruined!

Mother doesn't let very much get her down, but she looked as if she'd just been hit over the head. She was the chairman of the carnival this year—and the whole thing was doomed to failure before it started.

"Rides," Frankie muttered. "Rides?" he said louder. Then he shouted, "Rides!" and took off like . . . well, like a griffin in a tearing hurry.

"Don't worry!" he yelled. "I'll bring 'em."

Pat and I looked at each other. We were getting the same idea.

"Come on," I yelled. "Let's get down there!" I shoved Mother's purse at her. Pat grabbed Mother's hand and practically dragged her out to the car while I thumped Liam's carriage down the steps and ran it over to Ganshaw's. Mrs. G would keep Liam while we got things arranged.

Pat explained our idea while I was gone. Mother had the car waiting at the end of Ganshaw's driveway. I threw myself in, and we broke the speed limit to the town square.

None too soon! Right where the midway and the rides are usually set up was a gleeful-looking young Chinese dragon, all gold and blue and gorgeous. Mike, who is good at organizing things, ran over and directed the dragon to set up in a certain area. I waited until the next ride appeared—four centaurs, brushed and gleaming and hootin' and hollerin'. Centaurs are not quiet beasts.

"Where do you want 'em, Mike?" I yelled.

"Over here!"

Pat greeted the next ones: two Pegasi, who said they were the first of several pairs who'd be along soon.

A White Witch in a gypsy fortune-teller's costume arrived complete with tent, stools, table, and crystal ball.

Uncle Fran! "Couldn't let your mother down," he said. Then he leaned over and whispered, "I've always wanted to come back to a Halloween carnival. Had great times, when I was a kid. Besides," he went on, "I don't suppose any of you have bothered to inform your father."

I shook my head. Daddy was still at the store, getting ready.

"So nothing has been done about Wards and Bounds and Assurances?"

I felt as if I should go back and take my whole first year of Apprenticeship over. And Frankie should have had to stay home until he got some sense. We needed Wards to keep the whole thing from getting out of hand, Bounds to keep all the Magical creatures right here—they're naturally curious about Real and don't get much chance to see it—and Assurances to make certain no one from Black Magic or Nothing showed up.

Uncle Fran should have been really angry with both of us, but all he said was, "I trust that you will remember in the future—even if your considerably younger brother, who is also a Magical creature, should forget?"

I certainly would.

Uncle Fran strolled around, looking very casual but actually working very fast and very hard. When he had made a complete circle, he found himself the very best spot, sat down and smoked a cigar, and grinned as if he were younger than Denny.

A giant dressed like Hercules, lion pelt and all, brought a whole pile of huge barbells and other stuff he could use.

A troop of elves, the small, quick kind, dressed identically in gold tights with red spangles, marked off an area and positioned their equipment. Acrobats!

The lion tamer, a Master Magician, no doubt, had lions like no animals in Real. I knew none of them would hurt a fly, but they sure looked, sounded, and acted fierce and wild.

A whole bunch of strange-looking people appeared and said they were barkers, ticket takers, helpers, and whatever was needed.

At first I thought everyone in Magic had decided to come, and we'd never have room enough. Why didn't Frankie have some sense? Then I stopped worrying and tried to help Mike. Mother had caught on at once, greeted several of the acts with grateful enthusiasm, then went back home to get Liam and Mrs. G.

We didn't see how we could bring order out of chaos in time, but we actually did! At five o'clock by the town clock in the courthouse tower, the carnival opened.

Nobody—but *nobody*—was disappointed in the rides.

At the carnival, Daddy always puts on his Master Magician's robes and performs a Magic show the like of which has never been seen outside Kenrad. I'm his assistant, and we do one show each hour—which makes six shows and is a lot of work, but fun—so I didn't think I'd get much chance to ride. For the first time, I wished somebody else would help Daddy. I wanted to see all the other shows, too, and ride every creature who'd take me.

When Daddy arrived, Miss Carothers and a friend of hers who is also a White Witch came with him. They were dressed for the assistant's part and looked really gorgeous.

"I'll do the first show for you, Bridgie," Miss Carothers said. "April will do the seven o'clock. You get the six o'clock and the eight o'clock. We'll do the rest."

I kissed everybody in sight and rushed out.

I didn't know where to start!

The blue-and-gold Chinese dragon had been joined by a red-and-silver friend. They were nearest. Seats were strapped all along their backs so they could carry lots of kids at once. I managed to get the very last seat. They swam up into the air and made circles around and around like a merry-go-round, then up and down like a Ferris wheel. Then they snaked and curved and wiggled in several directions at once. Oh, was that marvelous! I suppose we'd all have been sick if they hadn't been Magical, and the little kids would have been scared to death. As it was, we were all just scared enough to have fun. Nobody wanted to come down.

Something on the ground next, I thought, and looked for the centaurs. Six of them now, I discovered, and they were racing! The kid on the winner got another ride. Mine didn't win, but I sure loved riding him.

I wanted to ride Frankie or Uncle Fran, but the line was so long that I decided I'd wait till later. They were dogfighting right over the square. Each of them took six kids at a time. Each kid got a Magical flashlight with a beam of a different color. If he hit the other griffin, a spot of colored light stayed on the target until after they were down. If the light beam hit anything else, it didn't matter. They'd count the hits and find out who won. The winner was declared an Ace and got

another ride. I had a feeling that a lot of men standing around were going to ride after the kids had to go home. They were saying things like "Lost Patrol" and "Wings over Wheresit."

Mike was in line at the strong man's show. He waved to me and held up two fingers. He'd buy me a ticket, too, and I could pay him back later. I know most brothers won't do something like that, and I'm very lucky. He was with a lot of his friends, but by now they're used to him including his family.

That was fun! Hercules lifted giant weights that took three or four other people to even pick up. He bent steel bars. He tore three huge telephone books in half, all at once. He held up a whole dozen kids—one of them me—at the same time.

He was bowing to the applause when a couple of the local men who think they're really strong, and are, I guess, stood up and challenged Hercules to a wrestling match. He agreed. The men pulled off their shirts and pants, and everybody knew they'd come prepared, because they had on swimming trunks. The first man really strutted up to the ring. Hercules let him put on a show, but it didn't take long—maybe a couple of minutes—before the man was flat on his back. The next man didn't look quite so confident, and he was down even sooner. They're not all that popular because they're bullies, and the audience sure let them know how they felt. That made the men really mad. They charged into the ring and ganged up on Hercules, who tossed them both right over the ropes into the crowd! You should have heard the yelling then!

I didn't visit the fortune-teller. It wouldn't be as much fun for me because I know too much about it. Most of my friends went, and they told me how fabulous she was and what great futures they were going to have.

The acrobats included a lot of things people can't do, like staying up in the air for minutes at a time and disappearing at the top of a toss, only to reappear somewhere else. All my friends who take gymnastics were green with envy, but they had just as good a time as I did.

I found Patricia Anderson, my best friend, and Marni Lewis, and we went together to ride the Pegasi. Two riders to a beast meant we had to look up another friend, but that was no problem. The moment we were off the ground, I knew they'd taken us to a Special Place. Magical creatures can't take people to Magic, but they can create a sort of dreamworld. I don't know if we disappeared or just seemed to ride slowly around the carnival grounds, but we didn't notice anything but the dream at the time.

Each of us had her own dream, and mine was so special that I want to keep it inside forever. I knew the other girls felt the same way, because we didn't talk much when we got down. I hoped they'd be able to remember. Magic fades for un-Magicals.

Marni's a dancer and is going to be a ballet star when she grows up. So she says, and I think she will. She practices four hours a day and goes into the city for lessons once a week. She insisted we all go watch the dancing.

A group of Light Elves, the tall, slim, mysterious-looking kind, wore beautiful costumes. They had brought their own musicians, and they danced on, around, over, and through the bandstand. Marni looked enchanted, and maybe she was, a little. Of course, she couldn't ever do some of the things they did, but if the Good Spell took, she could learn the feel and the wonderful movements and if she works even harder, maybe someday she can show people how elves dance. Patricia's an athlete, and I expected her to be sort of neutral. No way.

We needed something active after that, so we ran over to ride Frankie and Uncle Fran. I didn't win the dogfight. I was having too much fun just flying. Patricia won, though, and oh, boy, was she going to let her big brother know. He'd come in third.

I didn't have much time before I had to be at Daddy's tent, and I was starved. Patricia and Marni had eaten early, so I yelled, "Come to the show!" and rushed over to get beans and wienies and salad and cider from the Church Auxiliary Ladies. Good, as usual.

Everybody was completely mystified by the Magic show. They cheered and clapped and stood up and stomped their feet. Daddy and I grinned at each other. Fun!

Sea creatures, in general, are pretty iffy about good and evil, so I didn't expect to see a water show. But nothing's evil about whales and sea lions and other sea mammals—or their Magical look-alikes. Other people seemed to think it perfectly reasonable to see a gigantic tank and bleachers at a PTA carnival, but I knew we went into a Special Place to see that show. Not only did the Magical sea mammals do things above the water and near the surface, but also all the water in the tank rose up about fifty feet so we could see them swimming and diving and whirling and twisting and doing all kinds of dancing and formation swimming. I think my mouth must have been open in amazement for a whole half hour.

My brother Pat found me and dragged me off to see the dwarfs. They'd come to show off their handwork, and some of it was for sale. It was simply fabulous—like nothing in Real. Everything was pretty expensive, but Daddy'd given us five dollars each to buy something. It if cost more, we'd have to make up the difference from our savings.

"Bridgie, I just have to have that," Pat said. He was staring at a construction of wheels and sparkles and movement that I couldn't exactly see. Real Magic, I knew, and probably Pat, even with his powers suspended, was the only one in the place who really could see it.

"Too expensive," I said. I was sorry, too. Later on, this would be right for Pat; it certainly wasn't right for anybody else.

"I've got ten dollars saved up. Mother said I could have all of next month's allowance except church money. Can I borrow the rest from you? Please, Bridgie. I'll pay it back. I promise."

I looked at the price again. "I don't have that much," I said. "But you can have my five dollars."

Giving up the spending money hurt, but Pat's not having the thing would hurt a lot more.

Pat looked at me as if I'd grown wings and a halo. "Oh, gee, Bridgie. You're the greatest! Sometime, when it's important to you, I'll help."

He would, too. That made me feel a little better.

We rushed off to find Daddy between shows and get the rest of the money. When we went back to the dwarfs' tent, of course the thing was still there. Pat clutched the sack as if it held his heart's desire and took it to the car. Later, when he had his powers back, he'd get to know it.

I stuffed my disappointment into the bottom of my mind, left the dwarfs' tent without looking at anything else, and tramped back to the Magic show just in time. Being onstage always keeps my mind off everything else.

Pat and Mike were waiting for me. We always go to the Spook House together as our last thing. The boys have to go home right afterward with Mother. I usually get to stay because I'm in the show, but I thought I'd go with them tonight. For me the shine was off the carnival. I was ashamed of myself, but I couldn't help it. I tried not to let it show. That'd spoil Pat's whole evening—and maybe a lot more of his life.

"Let's go!" I yelled, and ran off. They pounded after me, ducking and dodging.

The town museum is in an old house—the only one left on the square. It's perfect for a spook house. The drama students from the high school and the college get together and work on it for months. Every year it gets better. This year, I was afraid it'd seem second-rate because of all the Magic, but it wasn't. People can supply their own magic, if they want to enough. We sure did. We shivered and shook and yelped and screamed and ran and bumped into things and fell down on squishy whatevers and got covered in cobwebs with spiders in them and everything else you can think of. Oh, boy! Oh, gee! It was great!

On the way back to the car, Pat asked Mike what he'd bought from the dwarfs. I wished he'd kept his mouth shut. I'd had so much fun, I'd forgotten.

"Nothing," Mike said. "That kind of stuff just isn't my thing. I'll save the money for something else."

Pat and I stopped dead.

"Mike, Bridgie lent me her five dollars, and she really wants something. Can I borrow yours, instead? I'll pay you back, I promise."

"Well, I guess so," Mike said. "But before Christmas, OK?"

"Before Christmas," Pat agreed.

Mike took out his wallet and handed me the bill. I could hardly hold onto it, I was so excited.

"Thank you, thank you, thank you. Tell Mother I'll stay with Daddy," I shouted over my shoulder.

I spent one whole hour deciding what I'd get. Five dollars really wasn't enough. Then a thought hit me. I'd completely forgotten that Daddy always pays me three dollars a performance for helping with the show! I had six dollars coming! For ten dollars I could get a narrow silver bracelet with my Witch Name in runes! I tore over to Daddy, got paid, and ran back to the tent.

On the way home in Miss Carothers' little car, I cuddled up against Daddy and ran my fingers over the smooth silver, reading the runes with my fingertips. "Daddy," I whispered. He leaned down. "I really didn't remember when I first gave Pat my five dollars."

He hugged me. "I know, daughter. And I'm very glad that sometimes, even in Real, virtue is rewarded."

I wasn't quite sure what he meant, but he was still proud of me, and everything was very, very, very all right.

As the Magicals didn't want any sort of payment, the carnival earned more than it ever had or has since. But that wasn't the main reason nobody in Kenrad will ever forget the year Frankie supplied the carnival rides.

Family Camping

A STORY BY BRIDGIT O'RILEY

The next summer was the best. The best everything. And the best of the best was that Daddy took us camping for two whole weeks!

Mother was invited, but she turned us down. "I am going to take Liam to visit my parents. They've hardly met their youngest grandson," she said. "And I look forward to two weeks of being pampered and petted. No cooking over an open fire and washing in cold water for me."

"But you and Daddy go camping," Mike protested.

Mother and Daddy looked at each other and grinned.

"That's different," Mother said.

"Different how?"

Daddy leaned over the table and said, "No kids!"

Mike said, "Oh."

We all laughed. I guess even our parents like to have some time without six children. I would, if I had them.

Daddy spread a map out on the table. "Look here, campers," he said. "I thought we'd go way out West to that park I've told you about."

Getting ready to go camping is almost as much fun as going. We packed and repacked, and even bought some new things. We all had lists—everything necessary and nothing extra. We're the only campers in the world who don't have to take matches with us.

The morning we started was so confused that I don't see how we got away, but we did, and only fifteen minutes late. We did get Mother to the train station in time, but barely. Mother feels about trains the way I feel about flying. She said she felt like Cinderella getting into her pumpkin coach.

As soon as we'd waved good-bye, we all scrambled back on Frankie, and he set off for the park.

How anybody can go to sleep while they're flying, I don't know, but after lunch the boys and Daddy did. I was feeling too full, but I sure wasn't sleepy. There was too much to see. Frankie and I looked down on everything, and around at the sky and the clouds. We talked to the birds and just enjoyed the flight.

Late in the afternoon, Frankie broke off right in the middle of a sentence. "Hey, Bridgie, we're here. Wake Daddy."

I looked down. Sure enough, I could see the entrance gate and the lodge not far ahead through the trees. I leaned over and touched Daddy's shoulder. "Daddy, we're here."

Those magic words woke the boys, too. Everyone started talking at once.

"Look down there."

"I'm going to climb that mountain."

"Where are we going to camp?"

"Land outside the gate, Frankie."

Frankie landed in the parking lot. We climbed off a little stiffly and played tag while Daddy went in to get our camping permit and pay the fee.

When he came out, the ranger came with him.

"Thought you'd better meet Frankie now," Daddy was saying. "We plan to go well in and up, to the second pond. I imagine few people are up there for Frankie to frighten. But if you should hear stories about a small plane going down or a monstrous wild creature ramping around, you should know it's probably Frankie. I don't want you coming out with a search party or a high-powered rifle. Couldn't hurt him, but the rest of us aren't invulnerable."

He said that for Mike and Denny, I knew. Frankie, Daddy, Pat, and I don't have to worry about that sort of thing. Personal protection was the first power Pat got back.

Mother and Daddy have come here camping on their vacations lots of times, so they know Ranger Barnes, who's been here practically forever. Also, when Daddy requested the reservations, he sent pictures and newspapers articles so everyone in charge at the park would be prepared for us.

"Sufferin' snakes!" the ranger exclaimed as he looked at Frankie. "I had no idea he was so big!"

"Oh, I'm being a private airplane right now," Frankie explained. "As soon as we get there, I'll shrink down to about as tall as Bridgie."

"Well, in that case . . ." Ranger Barnes looked relieved. "I guess everything will be all right."

He handed Daddy a copy of the park rules. "One thing I want to warn you about. *No open fires.* Third dry year in a row and no chance of rain in sight. We couldn't have worse danger of forest fire."

Daddy turned to Frankie. "That goes double and triple for you, Frankie. *No* breathing fire except to start the camp stove, and only when I tell you to."

Frankie nodded. He turned to the ranger. "And when my fire goes out, it goes out. No danger."

Ranger Barnes laughed. "You'll do, Frankie."

From the air, we could see the small lake Daddy had called the second pond. If we'd had to pack in, even with ponies, it would have been a two-day trip through pretty rugged country. Easy to see why there weren't many other campers in that area. We could swim and fish and paddle in our inflatable raft. The inlet stream curled around a point of land where the trees weren't as thick. A perfect place to camp.

"Over there, on the far side near the inlet," Daddy directed.

Frankie barely had room. Not even a very small helicopter could have threaded its way through the treetops, but Frankie made it neatly.

We all tumbled off and stretched.

"All right, campers, let's camp," Daddy said.

As soon as Frankie was unloaded, he went over under a tree and went to sleep. "Don't anybody wake me till dinnertime," he muttered.

I love camping.

The morning of our last day, we all woke up feeling funny.

"There is going to be one pip of an electrical storm," Daddy told us as we got breakfast. "I'm seriously considering leaving at once."

"Why, Daddy?" we wanted to know. We were all ready for rain, tents trenched and everything. "It'll be fun. Let's stay!"

"It'll be fun only as long as lightning doesn't strike near here," Daddy warned.

"Because it could start a forest fire?" I asked.

"*Would*, Bridgie," Daddy corrected.

"But Daddy," Pat protested. "What's the good of having a Magician for a father if we never take advantage of it?"

Daddy chuckled. That's his usual reaction when Pat sounds as if he were twenty-seven instead of seven. "I guess you're right. I may be making a mountain out of a molehill. We'll stay for a while anyway, and see how things progress."

We all yelled.

If you're like our family at all, you feel peculiar before a storm. Some people feel uncomfortable. They get angry or jumpy. We all feel great. Everyone rushes around pulling silly tricks, and everyone else laughs. We had a fabulous morning.

Early in the afternoon we were all standing on the end of the point of land and looking over the water. We watched the clouds gather on the horizon. Far-away lightning began to spark between the clouds, then down. Around us, the air wasn't moving at all, and everything felt as if it was waiting.

Then the lightning wasn't as far away, and the thunder, instead of being a soft, distant roar, got louder and closer. The clouds rushed toward us.

Without any warning, a hot, smoke-filled wind rushed at us so hard that waves actually piled up in the lake.

Daddy pulled his collapsible wand out of his shirt pocket and snapped it out full length. He raised it as if it were an umbrella. It was, in a way, but now it acted like a lightning rod. Anybody but Daddy would have been burned to a cinder by the great bolt of electric fire that lanced down and reflected up into the sudden, astounding darkness of a huge cloud.

We screamed.

"That's it!" Daddy said. "Back to camp, fast. We're getting out."

We ran. Daddy pointed his wand and muttered Spells. All the tents popped down and folded themselves. Our things flew into packs. The sleeping bags rolled up. The air mattresses and the inflatable boats flattened out and flipped over into squares. The food locker dropped from the tree. Fishing poles unstrung themselves and snapped apart. The reels screamed as the lines wound up. In a fingersnap, everything was packed and stowed on Frankie. He'd taken the split second to grow. One more Spell from Daddy and we were on Frankie, too. He was already in the air.

"Down to the lodge, son. Make it fast," Daddy directed. His voice matched his face—grim. "When we get the youngsters settled, we'll come back and see what we can do."

The boys and I set up a real howl. If Frankie could help, why couldn't we?

"Can you go into a fire without being harmed? Frankie can. I can. Use your heads. Now pay attention."

Daddy is rarely cross with us, so when he is, we do exactly what he says.

"Mike, you are in charge of your brothers. If there is room in the lodge, stay there. Otherwise, take the equipment where the rangers tell you and set up just the big tent. You will take one hundred percent care of yourselves, stay out of the way, and concern no one for your safety at any time. Do all three of you understand what I mean?"

They did. He made them promise.

Daddy turned to me. "Bridgit?"

"Yes, Daddy?"

"You're Witch enough to keep yourself safe. Very likely, you can be helpful. I'm going to take you with us. If you prove to be disturbing or not useful, you will come back to camp and do whatever you can to help. Understand?"

"Yes, Daddy."

"Michael, if she comes back, you are not in charge of Bridgit. Got that?"

Mike nodded.

We were at the lodge. Daddy waved his wand. The equipment flew off Frankie and piled itself up. The boys jumped off and ran out of the way.

Ranger Barnes leaned his head out of the fire tower.

"What can we do to help?" Daddy called up to him.

"I'll be right down."

The ranger took the steps three at a time. He carried a walkie-talkie.

"Fly me out there to find out exactly what the situation is," he panted.

Frankie slipped a ring of tail around the man's chest and plunked him down in front of me. I don't think the ranger even knew I was there. He talked right across my head at Daddy, explaining what he knew.

"With your help, there's a slim chance we might be able to stop this fire before it really takes over."

Frankie circled up to altitude, then flew like an arrow in the direction of the smoke. Lightning cracked around us so close that Ranger Barnes kept flinching.

In three minutes we were upwind of the fire and flying toward it. Frankie hovered so Ranger Barnes could see everything.

The ranger leaned over Frankie's side. He pulled up the antenna on his radio.

"Before you start ordering helicopters and smoke jumpers and water drops, give me one minute," Daddy said.

"Make it fast."

"I am a Master Magician. Not the sort you know. I can control powers you cannot understand in ways you cannot believe. What measures would you take if you had optimum conditions?"

"Can you make it rain?"

Talk about sarcasm!

"Actually, no. Practically, yes. I can cause the water in any nearby lake or river to ascend into the air and descend exactly where you want it. I can control the size of the drops from a solid stream to a mist."

The ranger turned a little white under his tan.

"Can you set and control a backfire from that ridge over there—" he pointed—"to the one over there, paralleling the firebreak? The wind's building, and we're due for a fire storm. No hope of the break stopping it."

"I can," Frankie said calmly. "How wide do you want it?"

Ranger Barnes pointed out some landmarks. The expression on his face told me he didn't believe any of this, but he was willing to try anything, anything at all. Frankie began to spiral down.

"Hold it, son," Daddy said. "Where's the nearest helicopter?" he asked the ranger.

"The park fire station, main headquarters."

"Call and tell them to expect one missing," Daddy directed. "You and I must be up here, in the air, so you can see to direct my part of the operation. Frankie will have to be down there, setting and controlling the backfire. We're losing our transportation."

A helicopter appeared beside us in the air, rotors still. They began to turn. When it was holding itself up, Daddy and the ranger disappeared from Frankie's back and reappeared in the copter.

"That ranger's having an awful time," Frankie commented as he glided down to our ridge.

We'd hardly reached our station when water began to pour onto the fire.

Not from the clouds. They stubbornly refused to do anything but spit lightning—mostly at Daddy and us, I was convinced, but Frankie kept me safe. I tried to act as if I was ignoring it, but I don't think Frankie was fooled.

"Gosh, I hope Daddy remembers about all the fish and things in the lakes," I said.

"That's why he started now, so he wouldn't have to take all the water from any one place."

Frankie flew low and began breathing fire. When he reached the other end of his backfire, he dropped me off on a big rock. "You watch this half. Get all the animals out. I'll go back to the other end and do the same. When my fire's crossed the break, I'll stop it. Then I'll pick you up. OK?"

I nodded.

I pulled my whistle out of the front of my shirt. It makes a huge noise if you blow it, but it's also a collapsible wand.

I worked Magic harder than I ever had in my life. I'm prouder of what I did during the next half hour than of anything I've ever done. Not one single animal got burned. That's hard. So many of them get confused or go the wrong way or don't move in time.

Frankie flew back and forth constantly, right in the flames sometimes, making sure the backfire was burning everything, so there'd be nothing for the big fire to feed on if it got this far. He got hundreds of animals out, too.

At last his fire reached the firebreak, burned across it, and took off all the overhanging limbs on the other side. Frankie flew back along the line, inhaling. As he did, the fire sprang into the air in a long streamer and flared back at him. I was scared to death, but it didn't hurt him.

He reached the rock and flopped down next to me. What an awful, black, lifeless strip of forest he'd made. It didn't even smoke.

"Great job," I sent.

He nodded his thanks. He was too tired to speak. We lay flat and panted for a while.

"What do we do now?" I asked.

"Wait for Daddy to tell us what's next, I guess," he sent. "Go to sleep."

I curled up against him and dozed off.

I woke up leaning against Daddy. "Is it out?" I asked.

"The last of it's burning itself out against your firebreak," he told me. "Nothing to worry about except the cleanup. Frankie and I'll do that later."

"Where is Frankie?"

"In Magic. I sent him off for food and sleep. Sound good?"

Oh, did it!

Daddy picked me up and whisked us back to camp.

Weird Doings

A STORY BY BRIDGIT O'RILEY

F rankie and I were out in the backyard under and in an apple tree. He was being comfortable, so he was about fifteen feet tall. It was a very lazy day, hot and sticky. I had on my old swimsuit.

"Is it going to rain by tonight?" I asked. We'd had a thunderstorm every evening for the past week. They'd just made the days seem hotter.

Frankie can't read the future, and he's not a Weather Warlock, so he really wouldn't know, but he shifted his Adam's apple off the branch he was hanging his head over and looked at the sky. "Looks a little like it might, over there." He wiggled his beak in the direction he was looking.

I felt too lazy to move, so I took his word for it.

"What did you do last night?" I asked. As usual, Frankie had been in Magic until very late. I'm already asleep when he comes home, so we catch up the next day.

"Last night was different," Frankie said.

The way he said it made me go cold.

He nodded at me. "I met Morgan le Fay," he said with his mind.

That's a name one does not say out loud. She's a genuine Sorceress. Prickles ran up and down my spine.

"She's dangerous, isn't she?"

"She sure is," Frankie agreed. He sat up straight. "You don't ever pretend to be her when you play King Arthur, do you?"

"Of course not! What do you think I am, a mental blank?"

We all play King Arthur when Frankie's in Magic. I always pretend I'm a knight, usually Britomart, since the only other females in the Arthur stories are impossible. Guinevere is unfaithful, Elaine is stupid, Enid is positively nasty to poor Gareth, and Morgan is evil. If I pretended to be Morgan le Fay, it would give her power over me. I wouldn't pretend to be her for anything!

Frankie relaxed. "You had me scared for a minute."

"The thing that bothers us is that she has so much power over Arthur. Mike says he can't figure out why Arthur doesn't just exorcise her."

"Because he can't. Arthur's Magical in a way, too, but it wouldn't work. If *Mike* were Arthur, he could. But I don't suppose he'd want to then."

"He doesn't really understand all that yet," I said.

"Me, neither. Uncle Fran says I will when I'm grown up."

"Daddy says that, too."

We shrugged at each other. Grown-ups get themselves in the biggest messes.

"How come Uncle Fran let you meet her?"

"He had good reasons."

"Start at the beginning."

"OK. I'll rerun it for you."

I don't need to, but it's easier to concentrate on mind-sendings if I close my eyes. I lay back against the branch and opened my mind.

★ ★ ★

Uncle Fran was taking Frankie to meet someone, but he wouldn't say who. Our uncle the griffin is always groomed to a gnat's eyelash, but he was making particular efforts to be dazzling. What's more, he insisted that Frankie turn on the spit and polish, too. Frankie, who thought he was all ready, discovered he wasn't and had to go through the whole grooming ritual again. Naturally, he asked, "How come?"

"The person you will meet today," Uncle Fran said, looking more solemn than Frankie had ever seen him, "is one for whom not a single barbule may be out of place. If it is, she will note it and find a way to— Well, that's enough of that. You will find out in good time."

Frankie caught the "she" and wondered if she were a female griffin Uncle Fran was interested in, one who was particularly fussy about appearance.

When Uncle Fran was finally satisfied that nothing else could be done to improve Frankie's looks, they took off for the North Gate. They exchanged the passthoughts, then flew beyond the gatehouse into Nothing Land, a neutral area between White Magic and Black Magic where neither kind works exactly as it's supposed to. It's not a good place to go as a general rule. We'd been afraid, before Daddy blocked his powers, that Pat might end up there. Strange creatures who can't make up their minds which land they belong in live there by choice, and so do some even stranger creatures who've been dismissed from White Magic or Black Magic. Frankie felt excited but not scared. After all, he was with Uncle Fran.

Far ahead, Frankie saw a tall silvery gray tower, perfectly cylindrical, with a steep, conical roof. He couldn't see any breaks in the walls, and he wondered how whoever lived there got in and out. They flew closer and closer, and he realized this was their destination. His heart beat faster. Something about that place drew him and repelled him at the same time.

Distances in Magic are always deceiving, and things often look the size they really are even from a long way away. So Frankie was startled to discover that the birds that burst off the tower and streaked toward them in a beautiful formation, accurate as the Blue Angels, were not birds at all.

They were griffins! Not griffins like himself and Uncle Fran, but the more common all-beast variety. Usually, Uncle Fran had nothing at all to do with them, but he led Frankie right into the center of the formation. When the griffin patrol had surrounded the two of them, they executed a midair reversal of direction with formidable precision and formed a guard of honor escorting Uncle Fran and Frankie back to the tower.

Frankie was beginning to wonder if he mightn't be the least bit scared.

When they were hovering over the tip of the cone, it opened like a flower with thousands of razor-edged, knife-pointed silver petals. He wished he hadn't thought of that exact description. Dropping down through the dazzling circle that could so easily close, skewering him with each of those needle-pointed sections, was difficult enough. To do it as Uncle Fran did, without giving any hint that he was concerned, was halfway to impossible. But Frankie did it, and Uncle Fran flicked him a glance of approval.

If this was just the beginning of their visit to whoever lived here, he decided he had better be scared. And alert. And very, very careful.

Uncle Fran alighted, flared his wing-feathers into a circle, arranging each feather with precision, and folded his wings so accurately that he might have been carved from jade. Frankie did his best to copy the maneuver and received Uncle Fran's approving thought.

Standing to one side was the most beautiful woman Frankie had ever seen. If he hadn't been so ultra-aware, he might have missed her very, very slight, subtle Spell that was meant to convince him he wanted to go on looking forever. Since he did notice it, he wondered why she bothered. She didn't need Spells. She was tall and slim and perfectly proportioned, gowned in silver-gray without a single ornament. Her hair was very long, a deep, deep red without a hint of orange, and the shimmers it reflected shone silver. The hair flew

around her in the wind of their wings, yet it did not seem out of control and dropped smoothly, to tumble like a live waterfall of dark blood down over her body-hugging garment.

Frankie wished he hadn't thought of that description, either, and hoped he had his mind closed tightly enough. He kept feeling the teeniest pinpricks around the edges, as if someone was trying to get inside without letting him know. He hadn't the slightest doubt that someone was, and the someone was Morgan le Fay! Uncle Fran didn't have to tell him what she was trying to do or who she was. He knew.

When Uncle Fran spoke, his voice was as cold as frozen silver. "As requested, madam, I present to you my nephew, to whom you may make your proposal."

Frankie knew right then that somehow the sorceress had made Uncle Fran bring him to her so she could ask him something—something he had to deny her if he wanted to go on being himself. He couldn't be prepared in any way, and he had to do it all by himself. Now was no time to be terrified.

He concentrated fiercely upon denying her the first thing: entry to his mind. If she managed to get in, she could make him believe he wanted to do anything she suggested. He went over every lesson he'd ever had in self-protection. Be strong, be flexible, be watchful. This enchantress had a million different ploys, and against them he had only what he was and what he had learned.

Frankie broke off the mind-pictures.

I was glad. I didn't want to know one more thing about that battle. I shuddered.

Frankie did, too. "Anyway," he said, "I didn't give in, and she had to ask me in words. She wanted me to become the captain of her griffin guard, to live there with her, and to take over all the duties she called upon me to perform. How she could ever think I'd say yes, I don't know, but she sure tried to make slavery seem wonderful.

"I said no as politely as I could, but I didn't leave any doubt in her mind. You know, Bridgie, when she finally realized she couldn't get me, she wasn't beautiful anymore!"

I didn't want to know what she looked like, and I said so.

"What happened then?" I asked.

"We said the most formal words of departure—no fare wells or good anythings—and leaped up through the center of the razor-flower just in time. Uncle Fran sent me ahead, and I'm not too sure he didn't fuse a few of those edges as dull as dirt. He sure wouldn't have left as much as the dust of a single barbule in her power!"

"What about the griffin guard?"

"I wondered, too, but they conducted us back out of her territory exactly the same way they'd brought us in—like a machine. Uncle Fran had won, and she couldn't break the agreement they'd made or she'd be moved entirely into Black Magic. She doesn't want that, I guess, though I really don't know why not. There must be some good in her, but I sure don't know what it is."

I didn't either.

"The instant we were outside her Wards, Uncle Fran thought 'Fly!' at me the same way you'd say 'Swim!' if you were being chased by a ravenous shark. We made it back over the Gate in about a zillionth the time it took us to fly to the tower. All the way, we were chased by gigantic lightning bolts and almost grounded by practically solid rain."

I didn't understand.

"She's one of the most powerful Weather Witches," Frankie explained. "She couldn't get me by Magic, so she was trying every other way she knew. Letting loose the worst storm she could summon might have worked if we hadn't been going so fast."

"Wow!" I breathed. "How awful!"

Frankie nodded. He fluffed up his feathers as I shook myself all over. His story had chilled me to the bone, and I was shivering.

Frankie looked around. He sat up so straight and so fast that I thought he'd knock me out of the tree.

"My teeth and toenails!" Frankie spat out. "Look back there!"

No wonder we were cold. The weather had changed. I'd been so interested in his story that I hadn't even noticed. As I looked, the sun was blotted out by the biggest, blackest raincloud I'd ever seen. The wind raced at us so hard that I had to grab Frankie around the neck and hold on for dear life.

He galloped for the back steps. I slid off and opened the door as he shrank. We dashed indoors. The wind pulled the door from my hand, and it slammed shut with a sound like a cannon shot.

Everything happened at once. The world seemed to explode. Wind crashed into the house at about a hundred miles an hour. Without Daddy's Protective Spells, a terrific bolt of lightning would have taken off the back steps. The door slam was a popgun compared to the thunder bomb that came next. A lake of water fell out of the sky.

Mother came running to the porch to shut windows. Liam screamed. The front door flew open, and Pat and Mike dashed in. The phone rang.

"Frankie, go quiet the baby," Mother shouted as she slammed down another window. "Pat, help with these windows. Mike, get the upstairs ones. Don't forget the attic! Bridgie, answer the phone, then close up the front of the house."

Denny was calling from Anderson's, where he'd been playing with Marty. They'd asked him to stay for dinner, and overnight if the storm didn't let up soon. Mother said yes, and we had one less worry.

I don't think either Denny or I heard each other say good-bye because another really incredible bolt of lightning struck, and the phone went dead. It must have hit the transformer on the telephone pole right across the street.

That storm was so much worse than any we'd had that week—than any we'd ever been through—that we couldn't believe it. We had to stuff old rugs and newspapers under doors and in windowsills to keep the water from coming in. Two trees in the field behind Ganshaw's were hit. The rain came down so hard that we actually couldn't see the street from the front window.

C-c-r-r-a-a-c-c-k! The biggest of the trees across the street fell right across the road.

"If your father hadn't protected our property, we'd be losing trees right and left," Mother muttered. She shook her head.

Daddy appeared in the front hall. "Everyone all right? Where's Dennis?" he asked.

I told him.

"Pat, get my camping poncho. Mike, can you find my winter galoshes? Bridgit, lots of old newspapers."

I stared over my shoulder as I ran for the papers. Why would Daddy get all dressed for rain? He didn't need to.

By the time I was back, Daddy had the poncho on, Mike was buckling heavy, high winter galoshes for him, and Pat was rummaging around in the bottom of the hall closet. He came up with the huge yellow rainhat I'd forgotten to take back to the school patrol room after school was out. It'd fit.

Daddy was going to get Denny and bring the Andersons back. In a storm this bad, the electricity was sure to go out, and the Andersons have an all-electric house.

As Daddy opened the door a deafening crash of thunder accompanied by blinding lightning stopped him cold. A horrible cracking sound filled the porch.

"Next door?" Mother yelled.

Daddy stepped out. "Ganshaw's maple," he yelled in. He was down the porch steps in one bound, splashing toward next door.

We pulled the door closed and ran for the kitchen windows.

Ganshaw's maple grows right on the property line. It'd been split right down the middle, and Mrs. Ganshaw's half lay on the ground. Our half wouldn't have stayed upright if Daddy wasn't a Master Magician.

Mother took a deep breath, let it out, and began giving orders. "Bridgit, ask Frankie to come down here, please. Change Liam and dress him warmly. Bring him down, and bring an extra blanket for the carriage."

As I ran up the steps, I heard her tell Mike to go to the basement and start the furnace, and Pat to make a fire in the living room fireplace.

By the time I got down with Liam, the front hall was carpeted an inch deep with newspapers, Pat was watching Frankie light the fire, Mike was pounding up the basement steps, and Daddy was coming across the front porch with Mrs. Ganshaw.

Mother opened the door, greeted Mrs. G, and listened to Mike tell her he'd followed all the instructions on the furnace.

"Good. Now go turn on all the radiators," she said.

Lightning and thunder! We all cowered.

The lights went out.

Nothing fazes my brothers for long. They charged around the house yelling things like "Great!" "Wow!" "Marv!" "Where are the candles?" I sat in the living room and tried to keep Liam from screaming himself into convulsions.

Daddy let himself out again, Mother and Mrs. G went into the kitchen, and Frankie worked a little magic on Liam—personal magic, not Real Magic. Liam thinks Frankie is the greatest. If Frankie told him something was OK, it was OK.

Things calmed down a bit. All that happened was that Pat and Mike charged through the hall shouting, "We're going to get the candles in the basement. Where's the flashlight?"

"Candles?" Frankie said.

That seemed like a dumb remark. As he's usually pretty smart, we all looked at him, wondering what he meant.

Frankie pushed open the kitchen door and spoke to Mother. "Where does the electricity come into the house?" he asked.

"At the meter box in the basement," Mother said.

"Pat," Frankie said, "go open the basement door and the door to the meter box."

Pat looked at him and ran off.

Frankie's tail started to grow. It got longer and thinner, and longer and thinner, and snaked out of the hall, down the steps, and around the corner at the bottom. In a minute, the lights came on!

"Frankie!" I yelled. "You're electrical!"

"Naturally!" Frankie said, meaning it both ways.

Mother took Liam from me and handed him to Mrs. Ganshaw. "Are you sure it won't hurt you, dear?" she asked Frankie.

"Positive," Frankie assured her.

"How long can you keep it up?"

"A week or so, I guess. My tail'd get sore by then, and I'd give people shocks if they touched me. But for a day or so, no problem. I'll just get terribly hungry."

I could do something about that. I started for the kitchen. Frankie followed me. I put his dinner down and opened the freezer to get out more.

"What happens when you go to sleep, or do you?" I asked.

He chuckled. "Asleep or awake, as long as I'm connected to the box, the electricity stays on."

That was a comfort.

Weirder and Weirder

A STORY BY BRIDGIT O'RILEY

The storm didn't let up for one minute. The neighbors noticed we had lights and began coming over. Soon we had not only Mrs. Ganshaw and the Andersons, but also about twenty other people sitting in our house getting warm and dry. Dinner was served in shifts, as people brought whatever had stopped cooking at their houses to finish at ours. We got out all the camping equipment and made up beds everywhere except the front hall, which was still too cold and wet.

I was running through the hall about eight o'clock when I nearly ran smack into Frankie. He stood in the middle with his eyes closed, swaying back and forth slightly. Little puffs of white smoke curled out of his nostrils. He was also growing, half-inch by half-inch, concentrating so hard that he was forgetting to stay small. Oh, did that scare me!

Nobody in our family cries wolf, but this was a real crisis. Mentally I called, "Daddy!" He was there before I could blink.

I waited until Frankie stopped smoking and growing, then slid into the outer edges of their mental conversation to listen.

The storm had caused a serious automobile accident. As a result, a little boy had to have an emergency operation to save his life, but the power was out at the hospital. Even the emergency generator there wouldn't work. Somebody there reported having seen our lights, thought it might be Frankie, and tried something nobody thought would work—*thinking* at him. It worked, all right!

Frankie opened his eyes. "Daddy, I can't help! I'm not powerful enough. It'll take Uncle Fran."

Daddy stopped looking like Daddy and started looking like a Master Magician. "I'll get him," he said.

We just had time to get to the door when Uncle Fran, like a huge black dream outlined in pale gold light against the complete darkness, splashed down on the front lawn. Mother ran out of the kitchen, hugged Daddy hard, and stood back. Daddy started to glow, disappeared, and reappeared on Uncle Fran's back. Uncle Fran leaped into the storm, a good power to the rescue.

"What's the glow?" Mother asked Frankie.

"Keeping dry," Frankie answered.

"Why is Fran here, and where are they going?" she asked.

Frankie started to explain, but he was yawning too hard, so I told Mother.

"Go eat another dinner, dear," Mother told him. "Then go to bed. You're exhausted."

Frankie nuzzled her. "Thanks," he said.

I went into the kitchen to feed Frankie, and Mother went to the back porch to get Pat and Denny and put them to bed. It'd be a lot easier to persuade them tonight than it usually is, I thought. Frankie would be up to bed soon.

Mike and I had so much to do that Mother didn't send us to bed. It was almost eleven when we met in the hallway and Mother looked at Great-grandfather's clock.

"For heaven's sake, youngsters," Mother said, "go to bed. Let's see. Mike, you may sleep in your own. I doubt anyone else would want to sleep in the same room with Frankie. Bridgie, I've put Mrs. Ganshaw in yours. Go cuddle up in mine. I'm sure Daddy won't be home tonight."

We started to kiss Mother good night when the very worst crash of all sounded as if lightning had split the house in two. The lights flickered, and all three of us nearly ended up on the floor. We were sure the roof was gone.

I had just enough time to realize that the lights, being Frankie-generated, shouldn't have changed. Then the most awful, despairing feeling poured over and into me. It was as though I could only half hear, half see, half *function*, and could no longer do anything by intuition, instinct, or habit. I knew instantly what it was. My Magical powers had been blocked off so I couldn't use them.

Outside on the porch, silhouetted against the next lightning flash, was a tall, thin shadow.

In the silence after the thunderclap, the doorbell rang. Mother went to the door.

I couldn't stop her. Not only was I un-Magical, but I was also powerless to do anything to protect us.

Mother opened the door. In blew a tall, slender woman. She was really beautiful, with shining gray eyes and long, silky, dark red hair.

She was! She had to be!

Morgan le Fay!

She'd come to get Frankie. Daddy wasn't here to protect us. I *knew* she'd caused the accident—and why, *why* hadn't we connected the terrible storm here with what Frankie told me she'd done in Magic? Frankie had said she was a powerful Weather Witch.

She'd probably prevented us from associating the storm with her, with the very first lightning bolt, the one that nearly hit us by the porch door. Otherwise, surely Frankie or I would have put two and two together before now. I wanted to cry, but I couldn't.

I stood there like a statue while Mother and Morgan le Fay had the sort of conversation you'd expect. "Come in out of the rain, isn't it terrible, thank you, my car ran into a tree across the road."

Mike took her cloak—*cloak*, yet!—down to the basement to hang it up, even though I could see it was perfectly dry. Mother offered her a hot drink and a place to spend the night.

All that time I stood there silently. I couldn't do or say anything except what Morgan le Fay wanted me to, and whatever that was, I wouldn't do or say it. Mother didn't seem to notice the way I was acting. She just showed the Enchantress to the kitchen.

As soon as Morgan le Fay was out of the hall, I could move. What was I going to do?

Mike came back up the stairs. He looked at me with a very peculiar expression on his face. Then he came over close so he could whisper. "Bridgie, the cloak wasn't wet."

I discovered I could nod, even though I couldn't speak.

Mike went on. "She's nobody from around here. She looks like somebody Frankie'd bring home from Magic, but she's all *wrong.*"

Excited, hopeful things happened to my insides. My completely un-Magical brother, funny, wonderful Mike, was going to figure it out. He was. He *was.*

"Something is wrong, isn't it, Bridgie?"

What could I say? How could I help? I had to do something!

"I cannot answer your question," was the only thing that would come out of my mouth.

"Why?"

"Same answer."

Mike looked at me even more oddly. His eyes narrowed the way they do when he's getting an idea. He's lived around Magic all his life. He was coming up with something.

"Who is she?"

How could I help without her knowing? I blurted out the only thing I could think of fast. "Boris."

"Boris?" Mike repeated. "But that's a boy's name." He stopped.

"Boris is Elmer's father's dragon," he said slowly, "in *The Dragons of Blueland*."

I wiggled my hand as if I were writing.

"Write. Pencil. Pen," Mike said. "Pen! Pen dragon. Pendragon! King Arthur! She's Morgan le Fay!"

He spun away from me and leaped up the steps two at a time. "I'm going to get Frankie."

I knew it wouldn't do any good. If she'd made me powerless, she sure wouldn't have ignored Frankie. And Pat, even with his powers suppressed, was Magical, so Morgan would have taken care of him, too.

In a couple of minutes Mike came downstairs slowly. "I can't wake him," he whispered. "Or Pat. Frankie's like a statue, and Pat looks as if he's asleep. They're breathing, but they don't even grunt when you shake them."

Mother and Morgan came out of the kitchen. Our guest had a tall, steaming glass in her hand. She was saying, "I'm too tired to care—and I'm sure I'll just be excited to meet such an unusual new friend."

Mother turned to Mike. "You won't mind Miss Morgan's using your bed tonight, will you, dear?" she asked a little too brightly.

Mike started to object, then seemed to decide not to. As Morgan hasn't that kind of power over un-Magicals, I guessed he did it himself. "No, I don't mind," he said. "I'll use the other end of Pat's bed."

Morgan looked odd for an instant. Then she smiled. "Why, that will be just fine." Her voice was so syrupy that you could have scooped it up with a spoon.

"Shall we go up?" Mother invited.

The three of them went upstairs. I trailed along helplessly.

"Bridgie, get clean sheets and make up Mike's bed for Miss Morgan," Mother said. She led the Sorceress along the hall to her own bedroom, I guessed to get her a nightgown.

In misery, unable to do anything else, I made up Mike's bed. Mike sat on the end of Pat's bed and thought.

When Mother came in leading Morgan, she was looking back over her shoulder, talking to the Enchantress, so she didn't see what happened. We did. Mother's parents sent each of us an ebony and silver crucifix when we made our first communions. They hang over our beds. They disappeared.

The expression on Mike's face changed. He went to the closet and got his pajamas.

"I'll change in the bathroom," he said. "I'll knock when I'm ready, OK?"

"Fine, Michael." Morgan's voice and smile had turned to molasses.

I heard Mike open a door and close it behind him, but it wasn't the bathroom door. It was the door to the attic stairs.

As soon as I turned back the spread, I left. I said good night pleasantly, but I wanted to scream and scratch. Morgan knew it, too, and her charm could have been cut with a knife. I wished I had one.

I opened the door to the attic steps. Either Morgan thought I was going into my room or she'd decided I was too unimportant to bother about. I crept up the stairs as quietly as I could.

Mike was in the corner, kneeling in front of the big green footlocker. He had it open and was searching in it quietly.

Oh, what a superior brother I have!

One of Mother's brothers was a priest who was killed in Vietnam. Our grandparents sent the footlocker with all his things in it to us because my uncle had hoped one of the boys might want to be a priest. One of the things in the locker is a crucifix, a big one.

"I've got it," Mike whispered. "I don't know the right words, but I guess God will hear me anyway."

I couldn't say anything, but I could still think. I prayed to St. Michael, the archangel. He's Mike's patron saint, and the Defender, and if anyone needed defending, we did.

Mike passed me with the crucifix clutched to his chest. He was muttering the same things I was thinking.

We tiptoed down the steps and along the hall. Mike stopped outside his bedroom door, took a deep breath, and knocked.

A voice inside said, "Oh, yes. Come in, Michael."

With both hands, Mike held up the crucifix in front of him. I opened the door. Mike strode into the room. If he'd been Sir Galahad, he couldn't have done it better. In the deep voice he used when he played King Arthur, he commanded, "In the name of the Father, the Son, and the Holy Ghost, *begone, foul fiend!*"

In the first split second, I saw-heard-felt a picture I'll never forget. The only light came from the shining eyes of the Sorceress. They lit the room with a gray-silver sheen that made my blood turn to ice water. Morgan le Fay wore Mother's prettiest nightgown. She'd half turned from an open window, dry and calm in the cold, wet wind that raged into the room. Her long hair blew wildly, black-red and silver.

With Mike's command, several things happened all at once. The lights came on, the window slammed down, and the boys' crucifixes were back in their places. Outside, the sound of the rain and thunder stopped.

A horrible expression, one of fear and cruelty and outrage, came over her face. She was not beautiful anymore! She looked like all the images of an Evil Witch that anyone has ever seen.

Then she was dressed in a long gray gown and cloak, her hair wound in a crown. She stood tall. One hand began to come up in a commanding gesture.

"Evil follower of Satan, desist! We cast thee out!" Mike ordered.

A shudder ran over Morgan. Her hand dropped. Then her nostrils flared and she raised both hands.

"Her name! Her real name! Call her Morgana of Faery!" I thought the words so hard that my head ached. But I was powerless to send, and Mike couldn't receive anyway.

Mike held the crucifix up before him and stalked across the room as if he were King Arthur himself. "Morgana of Faery, in the name of God, I command you to *go!*"

Just as the cross would have touched her, Morgan disappeared.

Pat and Frankie woke up, Mike clutched the heavy cross to his chest and slumped against Frankie, and all my powers came back with a rush like a dam breaking.

"Thank God," said Mother's voice from the doorway.

We looked over.

"Mother!" Frankie almost gasped. "Did you know?"

Mother came in and tried to hug us all at the same time. When we got unscrambled, she answered Frankie. "I knew she was Evil, but I had to ask her in. Then Bridgie turned into a zombie. You and Pat were worse. Of course I knew . . . something."

We didn't know what to say to that.

Mother went on in a minute. "Mike, how did what you did work?"

"She wasn't expecting it, Mother," Pat said. "She put Frankie in stasis, knocked me out for some reason, and blocked off Bridgie's powers. She thought she was safe. No un-Magical could harm her except by exorcism—and she *never* thought Mike would do that."

"He did a better job than you would've, even if you'd thought of it," Frankie added. "Mike absolutely believed it'd work. You might have let a little doubt creep in."

Nobody said anything for a couple of minutes. I know what I was thinking. From what Frankie said when he broke the silence, I guess everyone else was, too.

"Boy," he said to Mike, "am I glad you're around. People like me *need* people like you."

"Like us," Pat put in. He meant he was Magical, like Frankie.

Mike hadn't said a word. He sat with Mother's arms around him and gripped the crucifix. He got up now and looked down at all of us. "An' don't you ever forget it," he said. Then he grinned. "Guess I'd better put this away."

Mike was at the door when Pat said, "I won't forget, not ever again."

Mike heard, but he is such a good person that he didn't even turn around.

I won't forget, either, and neither will Morgan. She tried to get Frankie on his home ground, and *Mike*, unwarned, un-Magical, had sent her packing. She'd think a lot more before she tried again. Against O'Rileys United, she had exactly no chance at all.

Frankie Moves to Magic

A STORY BY BRIDGIT O'RILEY

I lay on the living room floor and stared into the flames in the fireplace. I was trying so hard to be peaceful and calm and reasonable that all I did was get tenser and tighter, and the painful, aching place inside got worse instead of better.

Mother and Daddy were sitting on the couch, holding hands and watching the fire, too. Denny and Liam were in bed, Mike and Pat were in their room studying, and Frankie was in Magic, as usual. The time was only seven-thirty, but it gets dark early in winter. Snow was falling again, gently, so all outside sounds were cut off. All I could hear was the sound of the fire—and my own breathing as I took a deep breath, held it, and let it out slowly, trying to think, *In comes peace, out goes tension.* It hadn't worked yet, if it ever would.

Mother moved behind me, and I thought I'd split open. She said, "When is Frankie leaving?"

I didn't move—suddenly, I couldn't—and neither did Daddy. After what felt like an hour and a half, Daddy said quietly, "Soon, I should think."

I knew it. That's why I was so miserable.

Mother sighed. "I hoped I was wrong," she admitted, "but I guess it's better to be prepared."

"He'll be back regularly for years," Daddy said. "It isn't as if this will be a permanent break."

I sat up, though I couldn't turn around and face them. I didn't want them to see the tears running down my face.

"I know," Mother murmured. I could hear the smile in her voice. After all, she was the one who had told Daddy about the habits of griffins in Real. "We'll miss him, though."

"Um-hm," Daddy agreed.

Nobody would miss him as much as I. Nobody could.

"Actually, Connell," Mother went on—I could imagine her sitting up and pushing her hair back—"the thing that's bothering me right now is where and with whom and in what manner Frankie is going to live."

"What do you mean?" Daddy asked. "He'll be with Fran."

"He'll be safe, certainly," Mother agreed, "if you mean he won't get run over by a truck or eat lye or some other such. But I do not consider Fran a suitable full-time guardian for a growing child. If he were a man he'd be a bachelor, a man-about-town. No household of his is a proper place to bring up a teenager, human or griffin."

"Well, yes," Daddy said, considering. "You have a good point there."

"Connell, before I agree to Frankie's leaving, you must go to Magic yourself and make arrangements. Frankie can visit for, say, a week and try it out. If everyone is satisfied, then I can feel easier in my mind."

"Think Fran will feel slighted?"

Mother laughed. "No. I do not. I'll bet you anything he'll be most relieved. He can just have the fun—teaching Frankie and taking him around to show off—without the constant responsibility."

I was beginning to dry up, so I halfway turned around to show I was interested in their conversation.

Daddy sat with his hands behind his head, elbows out, and stared off into space. "Think I'll ask to be a griffin this time," he muttered. "I've always wanted to. Never had the nerve to ask until Fran and I began working together. Think I know him well enough now to risk it."

When I heard the words, "be a griffin," I stopped crying altogether and got so envious that I turned a bright grass green. I practically jumped to my feet.

Daddy noticed. "Daughter, you really must control yourself better. Not only are you breaking your mother's rule about Magic in the house—though not by intention, I'm sure—but it is also not considered appropriate for an Apprentice Witch to display her emotions so obviously."

I only half heard him. Words burst out of my mouth. "Daddy, can Uncle Fran really help you turn into a griffin?"

He stopped his gentle kidding and looked at me with a very serious expression. "Yes, Bridgie, he can. It takes several things you don't yet have, but one day Frankie can do the same for you."

I knew that part of what he was doing was trying to make me feel a little better, and I let him. I lay down again. "All right, I'll wait. But you've got to promise to tell me all about it when you get back."

"I promise," Daddy said.

Two Saturdays later Uncle Fran came in after bringing Frankie home. I'd been to a movie with Patricia Anderson, my best friend. I was telling Mother and Daddy about the show when Frankie and Uncle Fran came into the living room.

Everything stopped, for me, and I went so cold that I thought my hands would drop off.

"It's about Frankie's leaving, isn't it?" I asked Daddy silently.

"Yes, dear. Hold on. You really do want to stay and hear about it."

I did, but I sure didn't want to break out crying in front of Uncle Fran. I started doing breathing exercises.

Uncle Fran rather pointedly ignored me, bless him, and I did manage to stay calm enough to listen. Daddy would leave with him when he went back tonight. Several families over there had said they'd like to have Frankie with them until he was ready to go out on his own. Daddy had appointments to meet all of them. He'd be gone about a week, maybe longer. In the meantime, Frankie would be in and out as usual.

Frankie and I would spend every second together, even if I had to pretend I had the flu! Not that I'd get away with it, but I'd sure try. School came in a very, very distant second to him.

Frankie knew how I felt, though he also was looking forward to his next step. He loves me as much as I love him, and he didn't want to be separated, either.

I can't say it was a satisfying week, even though Mother did let me stay home. All I could think of was, *This is the last time we'll do this*, even though I knew it wasn't. Frankie wouldn't be gone for more than a couple of weeks at any one time. He'd be back, and things would be OK. But I wasn't fool enough to believe they'd ever be the same, and I wanted nothing to change.

Daddy got back Saturday morning about nine o'clock. I'd been hoping he would come back as a griffin, but he can only be one in Magic.

"How did it go, Connell?" Mother asked after she kissed him hello.

"Very well, Kathie. I think we have the ideal arrangement. Remember that nice kid—the Chinese dragon—who came to the carnival to give rides? His family is exactly right, and he and Frankie . . ."

I didn't want to hear about it, now or ever. I threw the sponge into the sink, grabbed an old coat, and ran out into the backyard. Mother didn't stop me. She knows how I feel. Uncle Fran went to Magic when Mother was twelve, too.

I wandered around the backyard kicking chunks of snow and breaking a little stick into littler bits. I hurt too much to cry. My insides were so hot and heavy and painful that I got frantic. I didn't know what to do. Not only was I losing Frankie, but it was also that he'd be in Magic, where I wanted so much to go, and I wouldn't be able to go for ages.

Something I'd been hiding in my mind because I was ashamed of it threw open a door and stared me in the face. One part of me hated Pat! He wasn't born a Natural on purpose, but I hated him for it anyway. He'd already been to Magic, even though he didn't remember, even though he'd only gone because he was a nasty little brat and wanted to hurt us. When he got his powers back, he could go any time he wanted. I couldn't!

The other part of me started arguing. "Pat's not like that anymore. He's grown up lots. He's not a nasty little brat, and he wasn't very often then. You're being a lot nastier right now than he ever was."

Through my aching misery, through the argument in my mind, I heard a sob. Pat was mind-dropping! No, he wasn't. I must have been broadcasting so strongly that even Mother could have picked up what I was thinking. That idea didn't help. I got blazing mad.

"Bridgie, don't—"

"Get out of my mind! Go away! How dare you pick my brain! You're a horrible little sneaking snooper. I hate you!"

Poor Pat. Underneath, I knew he was just trying to be nice. He wanted to show me he cared how I felt and to tell me he felt awful, too.

Getting mad did some good. I stood out in the middle of the backyard in the snow and bawled like a baby. I was so *awful* that I wanted to die on the spot. If anyone had come out then, I think I would have. But I have a wonderful family. They left me alone.

I went over to the apple tree, climbed up into the bare, snowy branches, and cried all over the bark until I had a sore throat and my eyes were hot and dry and all I could do was gasp.

I heard a voice—Daddy's.

"Come on, daughter," he said. He stood under the tree with his arms up to catch me.

Even feeling as terrible as I did, I could see that staying in the apple

tree for the rest of my life wouldn't help anything. I swung over and
dropped down.

"Let's take a ride," he suggested.

I nodded. My throat hurt too much to talk.

He handed me a cough drop. It helped some.

We drove around for a couple of hours. At first, he just let me
cuddle up and feel a little comforted. Then we got it all talked out.
Talking about it didn't change anything, but I felt a lot calmer, and
I hurt a lot less by the time we drove home.

We got back for a late lunch. Nobody acted as if I'd done anything
unusual. As I said, I have a wonderful family. I told Pat how sorry I
was, and that envious or not, I didn't really hate him. I was just taking
my pain out on him. He got a little teary and said he understood. It
had hurt, but he knew what was happening with me.

"You felt the way I used to feel so often when I was too little to
understand, and I couldn't make things go the way I wanted them to.
Maybe it's a good thing, Bridgie," he sent. "I never understood how
other people felt when I acted that way."

"I wish you'd never had to understand," I said.

"No. Really. It'll help if I ever feel that way again."

Frankie left Sunday night for his visit. He'd be back in a week. I
held on to that idea and wouldn't let myself think of anything else.
School actually helped take my mind off my miseries. I studied as if
I were trying to enter Vassar with advanced placement by the day after
tomorrow.

The Saturday before Frankie was to go to Magic to live, I hung
around him trying not to cry until Mother couldn't stand me anymore.
She called up Mrs. Anderson and sent Patricia and me off to the
movies. I didn't want to go, but she didn't leave me any choice. The
activity helped, too, to my surprise.

Patricia isn't my best friend for nothing. The movie theater is in
the center of town, and that's two miles away, and it was *cold* outside,
but she walked me all the way to her house and let me talk. We stood
outside her front gate before she went in.

"Think about it this way, Bridgie," she said. "You're twelve. In only six years you'll be eighteen and can get your license, or whatever it is Witches get. That seems like a long time, but you'll have a lot to do. School, and growing up, and boys, and dating, and all that. And you've got friends here. Me, for instance. From what you said, Frankie will be grown up in a year or two, so you wouldn't be as close anyway. And maybe you'd feel left out."

I had to nod.

"When you get back together more or less for good, you'll both be adults, and it should work better then. You're not going to stop loving each other, you know."

Just what Mother and Daddy and even Uncle Fran had said, but hearing it from Patricia made a difference. I began to feel less awful . . . but a little guilty because since Frankie had been around, I hadn't spent much time with Patricia. But she was still my best friend.

I hugged her, thanked her, and ran the eight blocks home from the Andersons'.

As I puffed across the porch, I heard talking. Usually, I'd have called out "I'm home" in case I'd be eavesdropping, but I didn't have any breath left. I sat down to take off my boots.

"Connell, is there absolutely no way you could take Bridgie to Magic, even for a day?"

Mother was asking that? I sat stone still and listened.

"No way at all, dear. And, if I could, I wouldn't. She's too young. She'd be terrified. Things there are different. So different she'd never want to go again. Takes not only being a powerful Magician—or Witch— but also being mature."

"You're wrong about Bridgie, Connell, even as well as you know her. She'd be in seventh heaven. It would be different, yes, but not scary to her. She's done an enormous amount of growing up very fast recently, and though she may not be a Natural, like Pat, she's— She has something very special where Magic is concerned."

I was going to burst with surprise.

"I keep finding more reasons every day for having married you,"

Daddy said. "You're right. I guess I'm glad she can't go. We might lose both of them."

"We'll never lose either of them," Mother said.

I stood up, opened the door, and went in. They wouldn't lose either of us, ever. Knowing that somehow rearranged my insides so they only hurt a little. I could handle it. With a mother and father like mine, you can do anything.

On Sunday Frankie and I had a few minutes to ourselves before he had to take off. Everybody went away and let us sit in front of the fire and be together as the people we are now for the last time.

"Gee, I'm glad you're feeling better," Frankie said. "I was going to say I wouldn't go, but I guess I can. I'm not sure I want to. If I didn't know I'd be home every weekend for a year or so, I don't think I'd go."

"Oh, Frankie! I'm sorry I made it so hard on you. You have to go. It's time. And we won't grow apart. Just differently. It'll be all right in the end."

He nodded at me. "I decided that a couple of weeks ago. I sure feel a lot better that you know it, too."

All of a sudden I got an idea that had never occurred to me.

"Hey! Even after we're grown up, we can see a lot of each other."

"Well, sure," Frankie said. He sounded perplexed.

I giggled. "Didn't you ever realize that you could be 'Uncle Frankie' someday?"

Frankie gaped at me, snorted a little smoke, and laughed so hard that he had to lie down.

I was all right now. I'd miss Frankie, and he'd miss me, but someday I'd be just like Mother, having my special brother come back from Magic to take care of his nephew—or niece, if I got lucky. We giggled every time we looked at each other.

As Frankie and Uncle Fran flew away, we all waved, then we ran back inside.

"What's so funny, Bridgie?" Mother asked.

"Nothing, really," I said. "It's just that I thought of something that helps a lot."

"Willing to share it?"

I threw my arms around her and hugged her as hard as I could. "Sure, I'll share it. You did."

"I did what?" Mother asked when I let her get a breath.

I stepped back and looked up at her. I had such a big smile on my face that she blinked and smiled back.

"You had Frankie," I said.

Mother nodded and hugged me. Over my head, she said softly, "You're right, Bridgie. We *do* have griffins in our family."